# ROBBED BLIND

*Glimmer Vale Chronicles #4*

## MICHAEL KINGSWOOD

# CONTENTS

# ABOUT THIS BOOK

A stunning robbery threatens to bring Lydelton's economy to its knees, and constables Raedrick Baletier and Julian Hinderbrook must find the culprits.

A team of Royal Marshalls is in town to help. But they have an agenda of their own, and Raedrick and Julian must tread carefully to avoid revealing the secret of their own past.

With few leads and little time, the Constables will need all of their skill and wit to solve the case and save their adopted home from ruin.

Robbed Blind is the fourth book of the Glimmer Vale Chronicles, a mystery set in a world of valor and magic.

---

Enjoy the book! After you're done, please come to Michael's website and sign up for his mailing list at www.michaelkingswood.com/newsletter-signup/. Guaranteed to be spam free, he uses it to announce new releases and special promotions for his fans.

# MAP OF GLIMMER VALE

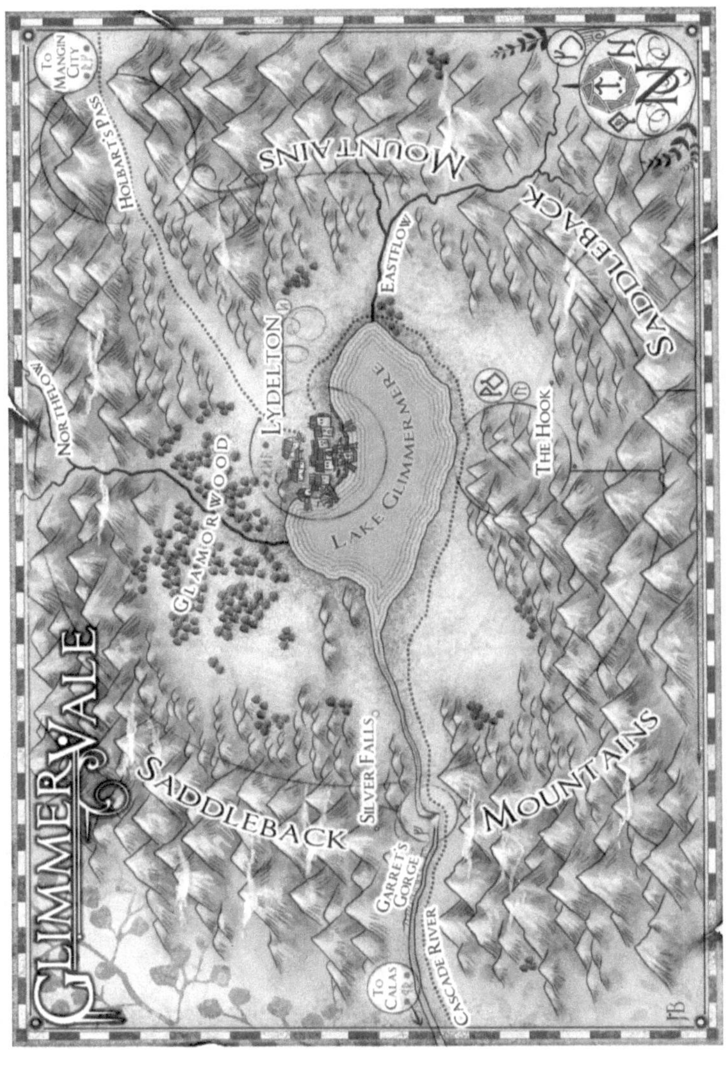

## FRESH ARRIVALS

The sun lay just shy of its zenith as Julian Hinderbrook turned right onto Main Street. A gust of cold wind flapped at his cloak and set his teeth to chattering, and he pulled the garment closed quickly, being careful not to upset the box he carried in his left hand. The rich smell of stewed beef and potatoes wafted from the box as he dipped his head closer, and even though he had just eaten his stomach growled in appreciation.

Main Street, the only paved street in Lydelton, was mostly clear, a sure sign that winter was on the wane and Spring soon to come, but from the biting chill of this day you sure would not know it. All the same, the last week had brought a welcome relief from the normally frigid conditions of a Glimmer Vale winter, and the townsfolk had taken to dressing down: only a heavy cloak and two layers.

Practically summer-wear in these parts.

Julian snorted at that thought and hunkered down against the wind, then pressed on. He set his feet carefully, lest his boots slip out from under him on the ice that still coated portions of the street, and for a moment wished he had thought to put his crampons on before leaving his office for the mid-day meal. But in truth the crampons would have done more harm than good, as little actual snow remained on the street.

He was approaching the turn to the side street where his and Raedrick's office sat when he spied a procession entering town from the eastern end of Main Street. He paused, blinked, surprise making him wonder for a moment if he were seeing things. But no, sure enough, that was a small but richly furbished carriage leading a column of four wagons, stuffed to the gunwales with boxes and crates, each drawn by a team of four horses and flanked by two out-riders

A trading caravan.

Julian glanced up at the crystal-clear sky, then around at the still large snowdrifts on either side of the street and the canyon-like walking paths that had been dug through them so people could access the various buildings. He shook his head. That was one determined group of traders, there. He would not have thought the passes through the Saddleback Mountains would be clear yet. Shows what he knew.

He stepped to the side of the street and watched as the caravan trundled past, exchanging nods with the riders and drivers as they went by. Finally, following the last of the wagons, a team of four riders reigned in in front of him.

"Ho there, Constable," said the leader of the bunch, a burly man in thick blue wool and a rabbit-fur hat, with a shaggy yellow-brown beard and flashing blue eyes. He had the look of a fighting man, and the grip of the longsword that hung from his saddle horn was well-worn from use. But the grin he flashed Julian's way was congenial.

Julian recognized him at once. "Marshall Leminster," he said, unable to keep the surprise from his voice. "We didn't expect to see you for several more weeks, at the earliest."

The Marshall rolled his shoulders in an easy shrug. "Thaw came early this year." He glanced around and chuckled softly, then added, "Though I see you didn't get the message on that up here." His smile faded as he looked back at Julian, and he became all business. "Got your pigeon, and I figured we'd best get up here to fetch your prisoner sooner rather than later."

Julian looked past Leminster to his companions. He recognized Job from the Marshall's last visit, early last fall, a tall whip of a man with dark hair and darker eyes who could spin a sword around like few people Julian had ever seen. He had a ready wit as well, and always seemed to be able to make the ladies smile.

The other two fellows were new. The first was a chubby dark-skinned fellow who despite his girth seemed natural-born on the saddle. The last man was...average. That was all Julian could think to say about him. The kind of average that could pass through a crowd and have no one recollect him. That could be convenient in his line of work.

All three men were bundled up for the weather, and had unstrung bows tucked into their saddlebags in addition to the swords that hung from their saddle horns.

They were all Royal Marshalls. Law men, but not the same as Julian and Raedrick. While he and his partner had authority over local law and order, the Marshalls dealt with Kindgom-wide issues of Law. Treason, conspiracy, smuggling, that sort of thing. And desertion from the Army. Julian hoped fervently that never became an issue, though it seemed unlikely he and Raedrick could keep their status a secret forever. The more they interacted with the law outside of Glimmer Vale, the more their names flowed around, sooner or later someone would see them on a list, and the gig would be up.

Someday.

But that would not happen this time, at least. The other thing the Marshalls did was oversee prisoner transfers, and Julian certainly did not envy them that. But he would be just as happy to hand them the man he had been nurse-maiding for the last few months.

He grinned back at Leminster. "I was just bringing him lunch. Want to say hi?"

Leminster pondered for a second, then nodded. "Don't mind if

I do." Over his shoulder, he said, "Job, get us set up with rooms. You know the place."

Job said, "Will do, Cap." Then, with a nod toward Julian, he spurred his horse and led the other two toward the street Julian had just turned off of, the street leading to The Oarlock and then down to the docks along Lake Glimmermere. No doubt that was where the Marshall intended to stay; it was the best inn in town.

Leminster dismounted his horse and walked alongside Julian as they proceeded toward his office building.

About a block back from the Main Street, it was a smallish one-story building with front-facing windows and a covered front porch. A small sign reading "Constable" hung over the door, but aside from that you would not know it was a house of the law to look at it.

They paused before the porch while Leminster tied his horse off at the hitching post that lay there—Julian and Raedrick took pains to make sure the post remained free of snow—and took up his sword belt from around his saddle horn. Then Julian led him inside.

"We've got company, Rae," he said as he entered, stomping his feet to get the ice and snow off his boots.

The front room was not exactly spacious, but it served well enough for the two of them. Its furnishings consisted of two desks that faced each other on either side of the room, a small cluster of chairs along the front wall, a rack of swords behind the desk to the right and one of bows behind the desk to the left, a wood stove in the back rear corner, and a shelf of books and papers near the cage-like iron door that led back into the holding cells.

Raedrick Baletier, Julian's partner, sat behind the desk to the right, going over some paperwork. He wore a black doublet that was lined with grey thread at the hems. His black hair hung to shoulder-length, and he kept it tied in a small ponytail at the nape of his neck. The last several weeks, he had taken to wearing a goatee to conceal a nasty scar he had obtained on his chin, and it mostly did the job. It also seemed to please Lani, Raedrick's special lady, very much. Julian would not have given odds as to which was the reason Raedrick kept the silly-looking thing.

Raedrick glanced up, an eyebrow rising on his forehead. "Eh?" He saw Leminster then, and surprise flashed across his face, replaced quickly by a professional smile of greeting as he rose from his chair and stepped around the desk. "Marshall Leminster! It's good to see you again."

"And you, Constable."

The two men clasped hands while Julian set the box down on his desk, unclasped his cloak and gave it a shake, then hung it on a peg near the door. The Marshall leaned his sword against the wall and removed his own cloak, and Julian took it for him, earning himself a nod of thanks.

"As I was saying to your partner," Leminster said to Raedrick, "I'm here to take custody of your prisoner."

"You're welcome to him. How long will you be in town?"

"Just long enough to warm up a bit and check on a few things. Two, maybe three days."

Raedrick nodded. "Let us know if there's anything you need while you're here."

Julian went back to his desk and opened the box. Within were two covered tins and a pair of spoons. He pulled one out and removed the cover, then brought it and a spoon over to Raedrick. "Here's lunch, Rae."

"Thanks." Raedrick sniffed at the stew and grinned. His grin faded a bit as he regarded Leminster again. "Have you eaten?"

The Marshall nodded. "A late breakfast, on the road." He raised a placating hand. "Don't deprive yourself on my account."

"Can we offer you some cider at least? It's been mulling all morning."

Leminster glanced over to the wood stove, where a steaming pot rested, and licked his lips. "Can't say no to that."

Julian said, "I'll get it, Rae. You eat."

Raedrick nodded and, sitting back down, set to his meal. Julian went over to the bookshelf, and from the top shelf pulled down three of the tankards that he and Raedrick kept there for this purpose. Then he filled them with cider from the pot and distributed them all around.

Leminster raised his tankard in a quick salute and took a big swallow. "Ah," he sighed, smacking his lips together. "That'll warm a man up."

Julian nodded agreement. "I don't want to think about how your trip through the pass went."

"Cold," Leminster said. "Bloody cold." He took another swallow, and his eyes turned toward the door leading to the cell block. "Well," he said, straightening his back a tad, "let's have a look at this bandit of yours."

# WELL MET

Julian removed the cell block keys from where they hung, on a cast iron hook next to the cell block door, and unlocked the door. Then he grabbed up the second tin from the box he brought with him from The Oarlock and led Marshall Leminster into the block.

The cells were arranged four on a side, and were separated from each other only by iron bars. Only the front and rear-most cells had solid walls except at the rear. Each held a simple cot and a set of blankets, a pillow, and a bucket for the prisoner's leavings. And nothing else. A pair of oil lamps provided light to the block, one on the back wall of the hall and one on the front.

At the moment, only one cell was occupied. That had not always been the case since he and Raedrick brought Geoff in, but even when they had drunks or others who they had to lock away for petty offenses, they never put them on the same side with him. Harmless drunks were one thing. He was something else. And with only bars separating his cell from theirs neither Julian nor Raedrick were willing to risk their prisoners'—their fellow towns-folk's—safety by putting them anywhere near him.

Julian stopped in front of Geoff's cell and set the tin of stew down on the floor, then pushed it under the cell bars with his foot. "Lunchtime, Geoff," he said cheerfully.

The bandit scowled at him from where he sat on his cot. Burly, with wild hair and an unruly beard, and only one eye, he looked the part of the ruthless brigand. And he had very nearly cost Julian and Raedrick their lives.

Well, Tolburt had. Geoff had just been the instrument. Tolburt was the fool that sent them to him.

Julian found himself grinding his teeth as he thought of his former comrade-at-arms turned traitor turned pathetic excuse for a man who Raedrick had decided to shelter here in Lydelton for some unknowable reason. Best to think of something else.

Geoff did not move toward the food.

"Suit yourself," Julian said. "You've got a visitor." He gestured toward Leminster.

Geoff shifted his scowl toward the Marshall, and if anything, it deepened. "Who the hell are you?"

"Royal Marshall Caperick Leminster. My men and I will escort you to your trial."

"Wonderful." Geoff's tone carried entire volumes of sarcasm and contempt. He cast one more baleful look at Julian, then he lied down on his bunk and rolled onto his side, turning his back to them both.

They left the cell block and Julian closed and locked the door behind them, then replaced the key ring. "You're going to have a fun trip, Marshall."

Leminster shrugged as though to say it would be no special trouble. "You've got the case write-up?"

From his desk, Raedrick nodded and patted a small stack of papers that had been sitting on the right hand side of his blotter for weeks. He finished chewing the bite of stew he was working on and swallowed, then said, "Right here, ready to go." He paused for a moment. "You know, if you could convince the magistrate to fully deputize our judge, none of this would be necessary. It would certainly be easier on you if we didn't have to transfer capital cases your way."

And that would also minimize their interaction with the outside world, Raedrick did not say, but he and Julian had discussed it a number of times. If only their judge were permitted to try more than petty crimes and misdemeanors…

Leminster snorted. "Don't have to tell me. But the money men won't hear of it. Have to pay your judge more, spend the coin to upgrade your facilities…" He shook his head.

"That can't be more expensive than running you out here every time something happens," Julian said.

"'Til you two showed up, we hadn't had a capital offense from Glimmer Vale in five years."

Raedrick's eyes widened and he opened his mouth, to object Julian was sure, but Leminster held up a placating hand and spoke again, quickly. "Not saying it's your all's fault. Things happen. But when you're making a budget, it's hard to justify spending that much more without need."

That was certainly understandable, but it was damn frustrating. Oh well.

Leminster drained the last of his cider and replaced the tankard onto the shelf, then he strode across the room and picked up his sword belt. "I'd best go get settled in," he said. He buckled on the belt and grabbed his heavy cloak and clasped it in place over his shoulders, then turned to look at the two of them in turn. "Join me for dinner at The Oarlock tonight? I've a craving for Molli's fried fish." His eyes gleamed as he said it, and Julian had the impression he could live a long happy life eating nothing but that.

It takes all kinds.

"We would be happy to," Raedrick replied, and Julian nodded agreement.

"At sunset then?"

Again they nodded, and Leminster nodded in return. "Until then."

Then he left their office, and Julian and Raedrick were left looking at each other for a long moment. A tension that Julian had not even realized he had been carrying seemed to melt away within him. Well, partially melt away that is. In his eyes, Julian could see Raedrick felt the same way.

It was going to be a long two or three days.

❧ 3 ❧

## DINNER AND A BAD STORY

The Oarlock's taproom was more filled than normal. Small wonder, what with the trade caravan in town. Townsfolk who otherwise might have stayed home this evening came out to chat with the caravan hands, hoping for a bit of news and gossip from the outside world, or for insights into what wares the caravan master had in store for the town this time, what deals could be had.

And of course, the drivers and outriders, packers and strong backs from the caravan were just glad to be in out of the cold, and looked to warm themselves, both with good food and drink and, mayhap, with a lively maiden from the town.

It made for a raucous evening.

Molli Millens, the owner, was in top form, roving the taproom floor and chatting up the clientele, making sure her barmaids were keeping everyone's tankards full and their plates brought out promptly. She wore her usual white apron atop a simple-looking dress that nevertheless had myriad colorful flowers embroidered at the neckline and cuffs, and brandished a wooden spoon that she used to chivy along any barmaid who appeared to be loafing.

Gently.

Lani, Molli's daughter, held court behind the bar, along with Rolf, The Oarlock's bartender. She took time to lean across the bar to give Raedrick a peck on the cheek when they came in, and to tickle his goatee for a second, leaving him flushing slightly. But then her waiting crowd swept her away and she was back to business, after leaving them with full tankards of ale.

Julian was glad they had patched up their troubles from earlier in the winter, and not just because he was fairly certain Raedrick would fall all to pieces if she left him. No, much more important were the benefits of having the Inn owner's daughter sweet on you—she didn't charge Raedrick for his drinks, and more often than not when she was serving that privilege transferred to Julian as well.

"I told you that thing makes you look like a scruffy animal, Rae," Julian quipped. "That confirms it."

Raedrick snorted, looking askance at him for a second before chuckling, "Do you see Leminster?"

"Hard to see anything in this crowd. Molli's going to make her next two months from tonight alone."

"Looks that way." Raedrick flagged down a passing barmaid, a slip of a girl with hair nearly the same shade as the fires in the taproom's two great fireplaces, and bent forward to speak into her ear.

She nodded briskly, then pointed over to the front left area of the taproom, and sure enough in the extreme corner Julian saw Leminster's telltale yellow mop.

"Thanks," Raedrick said, and slipped her a couple pennies. Then they hefted their tankards and made their way over.

Leminster sat with his back to the corner, with Job to his right and the two newcomers on his left. The table was, conveniently enough, sized for six, so when they arrived he waved them into the empty chairs opposite himself.

"Evening," Julian said as he settled down into his seat. He turned his eyes to the new Marshalls and extended his hand to the dark-skinned man, who sat closest to him. "Julian Hinderbrook."

Leminster said, "Constables, meet Iven Marpoli," the dark-skinned man nodded and clasped hands with Julian firmly, "and Bart Tiptree." Now it was time for Mister Average to nod, though he did not offer his hand. "They just transferred to my team from the Capital." He grinned. "Glad to get away from the insanity there, they are."

Raedrick nodded politely to them and shared his name.

"I hope you don't mind," Leminster went on, "but we've ordered already. I figured a round of fried fish for everyone, eh?" He grinned widely, showing his teeth. He looked a little flushed; was he that far into his cups already? Julian recalled that the man was a drinker, but not normally given to start so early.

Not that he was in any position to judge.

He was about to voice his objection to the meal order, though; the fried fish was low on his list of favorites. But just then a duo of barmaids swept up with laden trays and began offloading plates for each of them. In seconds, every man at the table was served, and the maids flashed quick smiles before darting away. They looked a bit harried, but who could blame them, as unexpectedly large as the crowd was this night.

Julian looked down at his plate and sighed. Too late to change things.

Leminster slurped down a swallow from his tankard and laughed. "I know, right? It's a shame to dig in, it smells so good. Makes me sigh every time, too."

Julian bit back his reply and set to eating.

The meal passed pleasantly enough. The two new men were quiet at first, but after a few minutes Iven piped up with an amusing story from his time in the Capital that had all of them doubled over laughing. The ice broken, he joined the conversation more fully. And of course, Job was his usual witty self. Bart, though… Julian was sure he didn't say more than a dozen words the entire meal. Job seemed content to sit back and let everyone else talk, while he clearly made note of every word and every motion.

That one was probably damn good at his job. Dangerous to be a wanted man around him.

After a time, Leminster pushed his thoroughly emptied plate away and leaned back in his seat. Fixing his gaze on Raedrick, he suddenly chuckled. "I just realized. It was about this time last year you fellows came into the job and caught that Isenholf and his cronies." His eyes narrowed, his tone becoming teasing. "And now you've got another bandit. You planning to make this an annual occurrence?"

"I hope not," Raedrick said earnestly. "Peace and quiet suits me better."

That went for both of them, though Julian did not feel the need to say so. The less attention that came by their little valley, the better.

"Hear, hear," Leminster said, raising his tankard to accentuate his words. He took a drink and smacked his lips for a moment before continuing. "Met with your Mayor today. Had to bring him some bad news."

Julian and Raedrick exchanged glances. "Oh?" Raedrick said, cautiously.

Leminster nodded. "Like I told you before, we basically hadn't heard from you folks in five years. And now, two capital cases in a year. Made people take an interest." He ran his finger along his nose, affecting a sly look. "Money people, if you know what I mean. They realized they hadn't seen a penny in taxes for a long time, and started doing an internal audit." He shook his head ruefully. "Told the Mayor he could expect to be seeing some tax collecting types this summer, probably."

Julian laughed in spite of himself.

Iven's eyebrow rose and he gave Julian an incredulous look. "Failure to pay taxes is serious, Constable."

He nodded. "Oh, I know. It's just..." He shook his head and chuckled again.

Raedrick gave him a long-suffering look. "When we took the job, Mayor Brimly mentioned that very fact, and that he's been collecting the taxes every year, regardless, despite many people's objections."

"And boy, do they object," Julian said. "You should have seen them last fall, when it came time to pay up. I thought he was a fool to keep collecting the money in the face of that. But," he spread his hands in a "what do I know" kind of gesture, "looks like the Mayor gets the last laugh, eh?"

Leminster nodded. "He told me that this afternoon. Showed me the strongbox where he keeps the tax receipts. That will certainly make things easier when the tax men arrive."

Julian had a thought. "Say, maybe all that extra unexpected tax money could pay for our judge - "

Leminster stopped his words with a raised hand. "Not likely. No," he said, "we'll probably just have to continue working with the system we have. Seems to be functioning pretty well, though it's a shame what happened with that Isenholf fellow."

Julian looked askance at him, then traded a long look with Raedrick. He did not understand that statement either. "A shame? I'd say he got what was coming to him. Hell, the gallows was *too* good for - "

The suddenly grim expression on Leminster's face made him stop speaking.

"You haven't heard."

Raedrick leaned forward, his expression deadly serious. "Heard what?"

Leminster scowled, but not at anything they had done or said, from the look in his eyes. "Of course you haven't heard. How could you have." He sighed. "He escaped."

It was like being hit in the jaw by a giant wearing steel gauntlets.

"What?!"

## ❧ 4 ❧

## ESCAPE PLANS

Julian realized he was glaring at Leminster, but right that moment, he didn't care. After all the strife Isenholf had inflicted on Lydelton and its surrounds, all the terror…all the blood…to hear that he had escaped… What the hell were they playing at down there? To let a man like him escape?!?!

It boggled the mind. It was infuriating, and irrational as it was, right then he felt the strong urge to leap over the table and pummel Leminster within an inch of his life for letting that happen.

Not that it was his fault.

Or at least, it had better not have been his fault.

Raedrick must have been shooting a similar glare his way because Leminster actually recoiled slightly in his chair. He glanced around at his men and coughed softly into his hand.

As if on cue, Job stood up and said, "I'm going to go get another drink. See if that barmaid from last time's still working here."

Iven and Bart traded glances, then Iven said, "We'll come with you." A moment later, all three of them were gone.

Leminster cleared his throat and leaned into the table a bit, his expression guardedly serious. "It happened shortly after I got back from my trip up here last fall."

"Last fall?" Julian said, exasperated. "What the hell was he doing still alive last fall? You guys took him in early Spring!"

Leminster returned his look with a hard gaze of his own. "Takes three weeks to reach Mangin City from here, Constable. And the judge isn't always around. He got recalled to the Capital for some business or other and didn't come back until the middle of the summer. And then there were other cases ahead of Isenholf's." He gave a little shrug. "It can take a while to get through the process."

Raedrick laid a calming hand on Julian's forearm. "How did he escape?"

"Well," Leminster drained the last of his ale from his tankard. "He pulled every trick in the book to draw his trial out. Even tried appealing to the crown, if you can believe it!" He scowled darkly. "We tried putting a stop to that nonsense quick. The crown don't hear appeals from deserters. But the judge made us submit the request anyway. Procedure. You can imagine my surprise when the request for appeal was granted."

"You're kidding." Julian looked at Raedrick, who frowned thoughtfully.

"Theobald used to complain that he should have been an officer because of who his father knew." He raised an eyebrow, questioningly.

Leminster shrugged. "Could be that's it. Who knows? All I knew was I had to get him bundled up for transport to the Capital. So I did, and I handed him off to his escorts." The scowl returned and he clenched his fists on the tabletop. "Couple weeks later, word came back that his escorts were found dead in a roadside Inn, and he was nowhere to be found."

He stopped talking, and looked at them, frustration mixed with embarrassment written all over his face. Well, he should be embarrassed.

"You should have told us about this as soon as it happened,

Marshall. He injured and killed a lot of good people up here, and he probably holds a grudge against the town. He certainly does against us." Raedrick gestured toward Julian and then himself. His voice was tight, coldly controlled, but Julian knew him well enough to recognize the seething anger that lay beneath. He was about ready to come over the table as well.

Leminster seemed to sense that he was on thin ice and raised his hands in a "don't slay the messenger" sort of gesture. "By the time it happened, the passes were already snowed in, and the only pigeon we had who was trained to fly up here had an encounter with a cat. Until we got your pigeon a few weeks ago, there was no way to tell you."

Was he serious? The cat ate his pigeon? That was the sorriest excuse Julian had heard in -

"But I really don't think you need to be worried," Leminster continued. "His description and the account of his deeds has been distributed to every town and hamlet east of the Saddleback Mountains, and there is a substantial price on his head." He shook his head. "He seems intelligent; he has to know we've done that. No way he's going to come back here, through all of that, just to pursue a grudge. No," he finished with calm assurance, "he's gone to ground somewhere or hopped a ship to foreign shores. Either way, he'll not bother you again."

"Easy for you to say," Julian said. "He's not out to get you." He shook his head. "You don't know this guy, Marshall. He's vindictive. I'd say there's a much better than even chance he's coming right back here this minute."

Raedrick frowned at Julian's words, then after a moment he shook his head. "He's not stupid." He drew a breath and put on his determined look. "All the same, we'd better tell the Mayor, and spread the word around for people to be on the lookout." He looked back at Leminster. "If he does show up here, we'll let you know." He grinned then, but his eyes held not a trace of mirth. "Could be we'll give you another reason to come up here this year."

Leminster looked like he was going to contradict their words for a minute. But then, he just sighed. "Can't hurt to keep an eye out, I suppose. But I really think you've nothing to worry about." He dropped his eyes to his tankard. "Sorry it took so long to get the word to you."

Julian blinked. He hadn't expected that turn-around. But then, Leminster had to know he was in the wrong on this one, and he always had been an upright fellow. Still, it was nice to hear.

"No harm done," Raedrick said, magnanimously. And that was true as well. It wasn't as though Isenholf had shown up causing mischief. Yet.

Leminster nodded. "Well," he said, and stood, pushing his chair back with a soft scraping noise. "It's been a long day. Think I'll turn in early." He lifted his index finger to his brow in a little salute. "Gentlemen," he said by way of goodbye.

"Good night," Raedrick said, and then Leminster headed off to the stairs at the rear of the taproom.

Julian leaned back in his chair and blew out a half-snort. "Well doesn't that just make your day. Makes you wonder why we even bothered."

Raedrick gave him a level look, one of those "you're being stupid" expressions he did so well.

Julian threw up his hands. "I know, I know. It can happen." He leaned forward again and tapped the tabletop with his finger. "But you know it wouldn't have if we had our own damn capital offense judge."

Raedrick shook his head. "Theobald would have made the same appeal, and we would have been forced to honor it. Odds are, he would have just made his escape elsewhere."

"Really? Who would have known about the appeal? You think Judge Telmon would have fallen for that tripe if he'd been judging the case?" He shook his head. "His head was on the block as much as anyone else's. No, good ol' Theobald would have been riding the gallows within a week."

"And that's why it's a good thing he wasn't the one to hear the case."

Was he nuts? How -

"If the judge doesn't follow the law, he's not dispensing Justice, Julian. He's just fulfilling his own bloodlust." He raised an eyebrow to emphasize the point. "Just like Isenholf did. The law says if he appeals we have to honor it, so we would have. You can't fault the judge in Mangin City for his escape, or Leminster."

Julian ground his teeth in annoyance. Raedrick was right, of course. But that didn't make it any less galling. "Well someone's at fault." He glanced over to the bar, where, sure enough, Job had three different ladies laughing at some quip of his. Iven and Bart were there as well, but it was obvious Job was the one the girls were interested in. "You can't tell me he just took down the Marshalls who were escorting him to the Capital all by himself. He had to have had help."

Raedrick frowned, and followed Julian's gaze to the junior Marshalls. "It's possible, I suppose. But that's not our puzzle to solve."

Julian nodded agreement. They had enough fish to fry in their little corner of the world. But all the same he couldn't help but feel a bit less confident about the system. He just hoped Leminster and his men would be able to keep hold of Geoff when they left.

## MYSTICAL CRAFTS

"The Earth Goddess' Wisdom" caught Julian's eye, as much for the illustration on the cover as for the title. He picked up the small, leather-bound book and looked, bemused, at the little animals cavorting around a tree that looked much like a woman, and shook his head. He flipped through a few pages and saw similar silliness within, and quickly put the book back on its shelf.

"Do people actually buy these?" he asked.

Melanie's voice carried over his shoulder from where she sat behind her counter. "A few. People gain inspiration from many places, Julian."

He snorted and turned to look at her, not bothering to conceal his bemusement. Their eyes met, and after a moment, her serious facade cracked and she smiled a little wry smile of her own.

He stood in the middle of her store, Melanie's Mystical Crafts, which lay in the northeastern area of town not too far from the Constabulary. The bookshelf was but one of the displays showing her wares, all mystical or supposedly powerful items and symbols that would appeal to the magic-seeker, or at the least to those who were impressed with superficial spirituality.

The store was done up well, he had to hand it to her. Words

and symbols of power, written in every color of the rainbow, were inscribed along the top of the walls near the ceiling. Some new curtains hung over the windows, their thin fabric straining the mid-morning sunlight to cast the interior with a warm red glow. Incense filled the room with a pleasant muskiness, and a wood-stove in the corner kept the place pleasantly warm.

And of course Melanie herself was the finishing touch. Tall, poised, and with all the curves a man could want, she carried herself with dignity and strength, and was always dressed to impress. Today it was a cream and blue gown that clung in just the right spots, despite being fashioned from thick wool, as fit the weather. It was cinched about her waist by a simple leather belt, from which hung the knife she always seemed to carry with her. In addition she wore a pair of silver necklaces and matching earrings. As usual her wavy dark-brown hair fell freely to just past her shoulders.

She was a sight to see, but as always Julian reminded himself that she was much more than just a pretty face. He had seen her stare down some truly horrific things and emerge unscathed.

Mages were funny that way.

"What can I do for you this morning?" Melanie asked, her tone of voice, deep for a woman's, conveying curiosity tinged with amusement.

He shrugged. "Just making the rounds, checking in." He moved over to the wall opposite the entrance and fingered one of the many pentagram pendants that hung from a hook on the wall there. "Nothing unusual going on here, is there?"

He could practically hear her eyes roll.

In truth, Julian was not sure why he had stopped in this morning. Melanie was always pleasant to be around... Well, not exactly pleasant, really. Agreeable. No, maybe that wasn't right either. Whatever. She was smart, and saw to the quick of things sometimes. She had certainly helped him and Raedrick out quite a lot over the last year.

"I guess I wanted to ask you…" He glanced back her way and stopped. She was no longer there.

How polite.

A moment later, she returned, stepping back into the room through a bead-curtain that hung in a doorway that lay off to the side, behind her counter. She was hefting a good-sized box, which she set down on the counter with a solid thud. Then she set to the box with her knife, cutting through the bindings that held it closed.

"What was that you said?" she asked, in between cuts.

Julian released the pendant and walked over to her, curious. "What's that?"

The last of the bindings fell free, and Melanie removed the box top. "Raedrick asked me to look into the note you two found in that cave when you brought Geoff in." She pulled a hefty tome out of the box and held it up for him to see. "I'm pretty sure I read that name Kalem somewhere, so I pigeoned a contact I have down in Mangin City. He sent these books up with the caravan that arrived yesterday. Hopefully," she set the tome off to one side and pulled out two more, smaller, volumes from the box, "what I need will be in one of these, and you two," she arched an eyebrow at him, "will be able to continue with your treasure hunt."

Julian snorted. "Not *my* treasure hunt. Rae can keep that fool's errand. If he wants to help Tolburt out with it, that's his problem, not mine."

She gave him that look that said she didn't believe a word he was saying. "You're truly going to let him go after whatever it is by himself?"

"Like I said, not my problem." He glanced at the titles of her new books and winced. "The Lineage of Post-Tribulation Man?" Trying to suppress a shudder and failing, he added, "I hope Rae's paying you to read that."

She rolled her eyes again. "I don't believe that for a second. The two of you are practically joined at the hip." She gave him a direct stare. "You're truly not curious about it at all?"

He opened his mouth to say yes, he was not interested. But her level gaze stopped him. Sometimes it seemed she could see right through him. He threw up his hands.

"Fine, yes it's intriguing. Who was he and what was that birthright of his? A fine mystery. But..." He groped around for the words. "Hang it all..."

"You can't bring yourself to admit it because that might mean you have to do something besides be an ass to your friend Tolburt.' She stuffed the cut ties into the now empty box and replaced the lid, then set it down out of sight behind the counter.

"He's not my friend. He's a backstabbing weasel, and - "

"And you don't want to let him be anything other than that. I hear he's been doing a good job over at Holb's, though."

He scowled at her.

The thing of it was, she was right. Tolburt had settled into the routine Raedrick set for him, working at Holb's Tavern until he had the money to repay everyone whom Geoff's band had done wrong, quite well from all appearances. Julian himself had not checked up on him—Tolburt was Raedrick's problem, as far as he was concerned—but still word got around. Most of it good, or as good as it could be, considering how Tolburt had made his entrance in town.

Didn't mean he wasn't still a scoundrel and beneath contempt.

Melanie held his gaze for a moment then sighed, put her knife away, and wiped her hands off on a small cloth she kept behind the counter. "Did you actually need anything, Julian? Because if not..."

As if on cue, the little bell over her door rang, and Julian turned to see a woman enter the shop. She was short and skinny, with hair that was more silver than blonde, though her features retained most of the shine of youth. Except for her eyes. Ilsa's condition was much improved since the death of her husband Baelin last summer, but she still sometimes had a haunted look about her. She seemed to be feeling it today, and even the cheerful colors of the spring dress she wore beneath her heavy cloak—and how could she stand to wear that dress in this weather, chilly as it still was?—could not brighten her expression.

Ilsa looked surprised to see him there, and stopped just inside the doorway. She actually flushed slightly and made a very shallow curtsy. "Morning, Constable." She looked at Melanie questioningly.

Melanie stepped out from behind the counter quickly, and smiled welcomingly at the widow. "Good to see you, Ilsa. Everything is in readiness, if you'll come with me." She gestured toward the beaded-in doorway.

Ilsa smiled, somewhat haltingly, then glanced at Julian again. "I can come back later if I'm interrupting."

Melanie gave a quick shake of her head. "Nonsense. I keep my appointments. Besides, Julian was just leaving." She turned her eyes to him, and that gaze screamed, "Weren't you." It was not a question.

He got the message. "I'll leave you to it then." He gave them both his best, most charming smile, and bowed low from the waist. "Ladies," he said, and turned for the door.

He heard a pair of low chuckles as he departed, and could not help but echo them himself.

## ❧ 6 ❧

## THE MOB'S WISDOM

It was not yet mid-morning, but Julian felt as though he was going to accomplish nothing this day.

His morning so far had consisted of his usual rounds of the town. He and Raedrick both tried to make at least two sweeps each and check on all of the businesses at least once a day. Not that he ever really expected anything to be amiss; Isenholf and Geoff aside, Lydelton was normally almost entirely crime-free. Even with the caravan in town. The drivers, and especially the caravan guards, were want to get into fights and the like, but they hardly ever caused any more mischief than that.

Ordinarily, an uneventful round through the town would have made Julian feel good, like all was as it should be. But this day… For whatever reason, this day it made him feel useless.

Damn fools down in the lowlands, letting Isenholf escape. Learning about that had him all in a funk. If they couldn't even keep hold of the bad guys after he and Raedrick caught them, what was the point?

Of course, that wasn't fair. But he couldn't shake the thought.

Going by Melanie's earlier, he supposed he had been hoping she would help set him straight. She was always good at pointing out when he was being stupid. Most of the time that was irritating, but today, when he already knew the stupid was strong with him, he thought it would have done some good.

Nope.

He trudged down the street toward the town docks, his head lowered against the morning breeze that sent his cloak aflutter, and scowled. It was shaping up to be a rotten day.

So naturally, he was not at all surprised to see, when he neared the Covington Brothers' warehouse, a veritable mob standing outside the building's main entrance. An angry mob, and getting larger, louder, and angrier by the second.

What in blazes was going on?

Julian's scowl grew until he felt canyons growing in his face, and he picked up his pace, stalking toward the crowd of men and silently hoping one of them would try to stop his progress.

As he drew nearer, he saw the focus of their attention: an older man with grey hair and a matching beard. He wore a weathered grey cloak over brown and grey woolens that were barely thicker than he would have worn in the middle of Spring. But then, Horace was one tough old fellow, who'd spent more time out on the lake than just about anyone else in the Vale. That's how he got to be head of the Fishing Guild.

Horace and Julian had become fast friends, back when Raedrick and he first came into town, and he had helped save their hides from Isenholf's band of brigands by convincing the Covington Brothers to let some of their employees off to help in the fight, at full wages. But he could be a curmudgeon, and he often got into quarrels with management.

What was that old coot up to now?

He drew closer, and Horace's words became clear. "They're not going to get away with this, believe me. They'll pay, or we'll have their warehouse down around their ears!"

Oh for the love of…

"ONE SIDE!" Julian shouted as he neared the edge of the crowd. The closest men jumped in surprise and turned, consterna-tion melting away into something that almost approximated respectful acknowledgement as they recognized him and backed up, into their comrades.

A general shuffling, accompanied by even more angry grumbles, started up as the crowd shifted, and for a moment Julian wasn't sure they weren't going to set upon him, just out of hairbrainedness. But then Horace caught sight of him.

"Make way! Let the Constable through," the old man said, and he made a parting gesture with his arms as though he could move the crowd by sheer will alone.

Horace being Horace, of course, he could. The crowd parted at his command, those nearest Julian giving him abashed half-grins and knuckling their foreheads apologetically as he stalked past.

He mounted the three stairs leading up to the warehouse entrance and placed his hands on his hips, giving Horace a glare that carried all of the frustration and irritation that had been building up in him during the day. "Horace, what in the blazing hell do you think you're doing?"

The old man stuck his chin out belligerently. Friend or no friend, he was never one to back down from a confrontation. "Those damn Covington Brothers shut their doors up tight against us, Julian. It's pay day, and they've not showed a penny to any of us. Well, we'll not have it!"

The crowd let out a roar of agreement and Julian groaned. He opened his mouth to speak, but the crowd continued on shouting so he could barely hear himself. Scowling all the deeper, he rounded on the men and bellowed, "SHUT IT!"

And then found himself blinking in surprise as the crowd not only quieted down but took two steps back en masse, their eyes suddenly wary, almost fearful.

It was then that he realized he had drawn his sword as he shouted, and he had to force himself not to wilt in embarrassment. What was he thinking, threatening these men, most of whom were friends?

He drew a deep breath and spoke in a more normal tone. "Now. I'm going to go in there and talk with them, see what's going on. I'm sure - " A grumbling started from the back of the crowd, but it stopped when he shot a glare in its general direction. He started again. "I'm sure there's an explanation, and this whole thing will be resolved quickly."

Julian turned back to Horace and slammed his sword back into its scabbard. "I thought you had more sense than this," he muttered, then he stepped past the old man to the door.

"They're not opening," Horace said.

"They will for me." He pounded on the door with his fist and shouted, "It's the Constable! Open up!"

A half minute passed, and then the sound of a bar being removed, followed by a latch flipping, carried through the door. Then it opened a crack and Julian saw a single green-brown eye staring out at him. One of the Covington Brothers.

"Thank goodness you're here, Constable," a deep but trembling voice said. It was Danil, the older of the two brothers. "We - "

"Open the door Danil," Julian interrupted. "We're coming in."

"We?"

Julian glanced back at Horace and gave a jerk of his head in the old man's direction. "Yeah. Horace and me. Then the four of us are going to have a little talk. Nice, quiet, and calm." He directed a glare at the old Fishing Man. "Aren't we."

Horace frowned, then, with a sigh, he nodded.

Danil swung the door halfway open and Julian looked back at Horace. "Make sure your people don't do anything stupid," he said. "And have someone fetch Raedrick." Then he stepped inside.

The interior of the warehouse was only dimly illuminated. None of the oil lamps were lit, and many of the shades were drawn over the windows, leaving the various tools, crates, dollies, and other implements of the trade cast in long shadows. It had an oppressive feel.

And, of course, it stank to high heaven.

Danil stood behind the door, fidgeting mightily and with a stricken expression on his face. Though he was the older of the two brothers, he was small, with thinning brown hair and a scrawny mustache. His clothing was well-cut and made from fine wool, his boots shiny despite having been worn through the slush on the streets outside earlier. But despite his fine apparel, he had the look of a man who was staring the poor-house straight in the eye.

Julian stepped clear, and a moment later Horace joined him within. Danil shut the door firmly and set the latch, then placed a stout wooden bar in place, before turning back to face them.

"Alright, Danil, what's going on?" Julian said, giving him the same level of glare he had treated Horace to a moment ago.

Danil shook his head. "It's terrible, Constable." He gestured for them to follow him, then he scampered off across the open space of the warehouse to the offices on the far side.

Julian followed, pausing only to give Horace a look of warning. "Let me do the talking."

Horace frowned again, but did not object.

The office area was lit by a single lamp that hung just inside the doorway from the work floor. As he stepped inside, Julian immediately grasped the problem, and his stomach dropped through the bottom of his belly.

Danil's brother, Jakob, lay sprawled on the floor near a large desk that sat off to the right. A wad of rag rested precariously on his head, soaked red. A trickle of blood ran down the side of his face from beneath the rag. His loose white shirt was already stained red extensively on the shoulder and down his entire left side. More blood had pooled on the floor around his body, but it looked older, like it had been there for a while. Though his eyes were open, he had a dazed, sightless expression on his face and his mouth was partway open, his jaw slack.

To the left, across from the desk, stood a massive safe. Its door lay to the side, its hinges apparently broken. The interior was empty.

Danil gestured to his brother, then the safe, and said, despairingly, "We've been robbed."

# 7

# CRIME SCENE

Master Sebastini finished looking at the gash in Jakob's temple and frowned, clearly not liking what he saw. He looked away from the wound, back at Raedrick and Julian, and his expression made Julian feel a little twinge of dread.

"It's a miracle he's alive," Sebastini said. He was an old man, older than Horace by a number of years, and thin. He wore the white and yellow of the Healer's Circle, and had been their senior Guildsman in Lydelton for decades. Frail though he looked, Julian knew him to be a tough customer; he had proved that earlier this winter when he went with Julian and Raedrick into the mountains, and met Geoff. "I've seen men killed from lesser blows."

Jakob remained on the floor, but at least he was sitting up now and had been since Sebastini arrived, a few minutes after Raedrick did. As soon as he saw the situation, Horace had dispatched some of his men to retrieve Sebastini, then sent the rest of them packing. The news of what had happened had apparently calmed the mob quickly, and they dispersed without further incident.

Not that there should have been an incident to begin with. What had Horace been thinking?

But that could wait.

Jakob still looked dazed, and he had not said a word since Julian had first arrived; he just let out a wordless groan from time to time.

"Is he going to be ok?" Danil asked, plaintively.

Sebastini shook his head and shrugged. "I do not know. If I had gotten here sooner…" He spread his hands helplessly.

Raedrick's frown mirrored Julian's own, he was sure. He looked with pity at Jakob for a long moment, then turned his eyes back to Danil. "Tell us what happened."

Danil ran his hand over his brow, clearly distraught. "He always comes in early on pay day, to make sure there are no problems. This time of year we don't open the warehouse until late, but he still left before dawn. When I hadn't heard from him by full light, I grew concerned, so I came over. There was already a small crowd outside, and they demanded to know why he hadn't brought their pay out yet. That made me even more concerned, so I came in to see…" He broke off, his expression tightening as he clearly was struggling not to break down then and there.

"I don't understand," Julian said. "Pay day? The lake's still frozen over. No one's going out on the boats for weeks still." He looked over at Horace questioningly.

Horace sat on a stool near the office door, looking thoroughly miserable. Probably felt like an ass, and it served him right. He perked up a bit when Julian asked the question, though. "They pay us year-round. We worked it out a few years ago. It makes for less money each pay day, but it stops my men from going months without any income during the winter."

"But your men take jobs clearing the roads and such," Raedrick said.

Horace shrugged. "Some do. But that's not always steady work, and don't pay that well. 'Specially not for a man with a family to feed."

Julian supposed that made sense. He looked back at Danil, who had gotten himself back under control, and gestured for him to continue.

"When I came in, Jakob was lying on the floor in a pool of blood, and the safe..." He gestured at the broken safe. "Well, you see. At first, I thought he was dead, but then he started moving. I tried to get him to his feet, but he was groggy and..." He ran his hand through what remained of his hair. "I didn't know what to do! The money was gone, he was hurt, and people began pounding on the door demanding their money..."

Horace shook his head. "Damn it, Danil, you should have told us. No one would have found fault in the face of this. But you shouted for my men to leave and slammed the door in their faces..." He spread his hands helplessly.

"I'm sorry," Danil said. "I didn't know what else to do."

Julian rolled his eyes. And he thought *he* was full of stupid today.

"Well first thing's first," Raedrick said. "Ravi, do you need help getting him to your Guild House?"

Sebastini shook his head. "No, thank you Constable. Willam and Heffi will be along shortly. They can more than manage." He pushed himself to his feet and turned compassionate eyes on Danil. "We will do all we can," he said. "With treatment and luck, he may recover fully." He did not sound terribly hopeful about that, though.

Danil looked stricken, but he managed a half-hearted smile Sebastini's way. "Thank you."

Julian looked over at Raedrick, who looked about as confounded, and hopeless, as he felt. With their only witness inco-herent, there was not much to start an investigation on. Unless.. "Danil, was Jakob able to say anything at all?"

Danil gave a little jerk and looked Julian's way. He shook his head quickly. "Just mumbles, and then..." He trailed off and made a weak gesture toward his brother, who had begun issuing another low, meaningless groan.

So much for that. Julian was not sure how to even start looking in to this, with so little to go on.

A few minutes later, Willam and Heffi arrived. Willam was a

young man with dark skin and close-cut hair who had been apprenticing with the Healers Circle for as long as Julian and Raedrick had been in town. Heffi was newer to it. Just out of his parents' house a month earlier, he eschewed the fishing man's life his father, Yorin, had pursued, instead opting for the path of the Healer. He was tall, lanky, and pale, with a mop of golden curls atop his head, green eyes, and a quiet manner. Both wore the white and gold of the Healers Circle, though their garments were simpler than Master Sebastini's, and they carried a stretcher between the two of them.

It took a few minutes to get Jakob squared away on the stretcher. Sebastini had to coax him gently, but he did not seem to understand what the Guildsman was trying to have him do. Julian had half a mind to move him, but Sebastini shot him such a glare when he tried to step forward to help that he put that thought out of his mind completely.

Finally, Jakob got onto the stretcher and the two younger men secured him. Then they lifted him up and bore him out. Neither of them said a word the entire time they were there, though Heffi exchanged nods with Horace, who had clapped him on the shoulder warmly in greeting when he first arrived.

Sebastini watched them depart, then turned to look back at Julian. 'Every chance he gets to use his own faculties, to think and act for himself, brings a greater chance that he will recover himself," he said, in the tone of a teacher lecturing a difficult student. "If we do everything for him..." He left the rest unsaid.

Julian nodded, understanding.

Sebastini smiled gently, then said, "I will keep you apprised, Constables. Danil, would you like to come with me?"

Danil glanced from him to Julian and Raedrick.

"We have a few more things we need to discuss with him, Ravi," Raedrick said.

Sebastini inclined his head deferentially. "Very well. We will look for you later on then, Danil." Then he turned and followed his apprentices out of the room.

Raedrick crossed his arms over his chest and directed a probing gaze at Danil. "It's safe to assume everyone in your employ knew today was pay day, and that you keep the payroll in the safe."

Danil nodded and opened his mouth to speak, but Raedrick kept right on going.

"Alright. Can you think of anyone who might have had reason to do this? Anyone particularly down on his luck, or dissatisfied with his lot?" He turned his eyes toward Horace and added, "Either of you."

"No," Danil said, shaking his head, "but - "

Horace frowned, but also shook his head in the negative. "My men have it tougher in the winter than summer, but they make do well enough."

Raedrick sniffed. "How much was taken, Danil?"

"That's what I was trying to tell you. They took it all."

Julian rolled his eyes. "Yes, they got the whole payroll. But how - "

"No. Constable, you don't understand." Danil wrung his hands. "They took *all* of it. All of our money."

Silence loomed for a few seconds, as that settled in.

"What do you mean all of it?" Horace demanded.

"Every penny."

"You mean," Julian could hardly fathom that this could be true, but… "You kept every penny you had, in the world, in that safe." He pointed at the once mighty strongbox, incredulous.

Danil nodded, and suddenly his complete despair became more clear. "We have a small amount at home, but only enough for a few days' expenses." He looked back at the safe and seemed to wilt. "Everything else was in there."

"Bugger me," Horace said, sounding poleaxed. "So you mean next month's payroll is…" He let the thought go, as though he were unwilling to give it voice.

Danil spread his hands helplessly.

"Son of a… I've got almost two hundred men expecting to be paid. Men with families."

"And forty more who work here in the warehouse," Danil said. "You see what I meant? We're ruined!"

Raedrick and Julian shared a long look.

"Well," Julian said, trying to come to grips with the problem as he spoke. "Maybe there's a way we can help your people muddle through until the thaw. Once you get a few catches in - "

Danil shook his head. "No. We need supplies. That's what the caravan was bringing up. New lines and nets, replacement sails. Preservatives. We purchase what we need for the season each Spring, and we only get enough for the season."

"Wait a minute," Julian said. "What about the businesses in town? Like Fedwyn's shop—he makes sails and things for you."

Danil shook his head. "Fedwyn does great work, but he's small. Most of what he does is repairs or one-at-a-time replacements. He can't produce the volume we need for an entire season out of his little shop. It's the same with all the locals; they're good for maintenance and replacement, but that's it. So we have to bring it in from the big producers out east." He snorted out a bitter-sounding half-chuckle. "I told Jakob we should keep more on hand, but he wouldn't hear of it. Had to keep inventory costs down. We were going to close the supply purchase tomorrow, but now…" The half-chuckle became a sob. "Now there won't *be* a first catch."

"Bugger me," Horace said again, and this time it sounded as though he might prefer that to what was happening in reality.

Julian traded another long look with Raedrick, and saw the same shocked comprehension as he felt. Fishing on Lake Glimmermere was the backbone of Lydelton's—of the entire Vale's—economy. If the fishing company could not do business anymore…

"This is really bad," Julian said.

It felt like the understatement of the year.

# 8

# BRIDGING THE GAP

Mayor Wil Brimly seemed to wilt as he looked at them. He reclined in the mammoth chair that rested behind his desk in the top floor of City Hall, and for a moment Julian thought he was actually going to melt away into the cushions, so badly did he draw in on himself.

Brimly was a plump man of average height who was well into his middle years, with a round face and dark hair that was beginning to thin on top and had already gone grey at the temples. He wore a dark green overcoat over a white shirt and black pants. A golden brooch in the shape of a fish jumping out of the water was pinned on his left breast—his badge of office as Mayor.

Brimly wiped a hand across his brow and swallowed. "This is beyond bad, gentlemen. This is catastrophic." His eyes betrayed near panic as he looked back at them. "You have to find this thief and retrieve that money."

No kidding.

Raedrick was more politic about it than Julian would have been, as usual. "We've already begun working on it, Master Mayor. But I thought you would want to know the extent of the situation, serious as it is."

Brimly nodded briskly. "Yes, yes. Do you have any leads yet?"

Raedrick shook his head.

That caused the Mayor to frown and fidget. "Well, get some! We cannot afford to - "

"Actually," Raedrick said, "that's the other thing I wanted to talk to you about. There is a good chance we may never find out who did this."

Brimly's mouth twisted into a scowl and he took in a breath to speak, but Raedrick went right through him.

"Jakob was the only possible witness, and he is incapacitated. We have not found any damning evidence yet, either. We're going to start interviewing potential suspects, but there are not that many to choose from." He glanced aside at Julian, pausing for a second before proceeding. This part was going to be hard for the Mayor to swallow. "You might want to think about what the town can do to help get the fishing company back on its feet."

Brimly shifted in his chair. "The town? Well... I suppose we could organize a special fund drive, or the like. But this time of year people don't have much spare money."

Raedrick pressed his lips together, a sure sign of annoyance. Julian didn't blame him. Brimly was not the most solid of men at times, but he was not a fool. He had to see where they were going with this; he just didn't want to go there.

"What about all the extra tax money you have stashed away?" Julian said.

The Mayor gave a little start, then harrumphed. "Out of the question. That is set aside for the Crown's collectors." He arched an eyebrow. "And I've been told they will be paying us a visit this summer."

"Master Mayor, you know what will happen if the fishing company closes up shop."

A reluctant nod prefaced his response to Raedrick's statement. "You don't need to tell me, Constable. We've got just over a thousand adults in Lydelton, and almost a quarter of them work for the Covington Brothers. That many people out of work..." He swiveled his chair around to look out the wide window behind his desk. Julian had always admired the contraption that let him do that. "It would be the death of this town." He suddenly sounded bone-weary.

"Think of it as a loan," Julian offered. "After the first couple catches, Danil and Jakob will have money coming in, and they can start repaying."

"This office is not a bank," Brimly said. "And I don't play fast and loose with the Crown's tax money." He pivoted halfway back and looked at Julian archly. "That's a good way to end up in a dungeon somewhere. A dark dungeon."

"I hardly think the Crown would object to using that tax money for something like this," Raedrick said in his most reasonable tone of voice. "There are no banks in Glimmer Vale, otherwise Danil could go to one of them. Preventing the impoverishment of the Kingdom's subjects - "

"The Crown objects to a great many things that we lesser men would deem sensible," Brimly said, with no small amount of bitterness. He shook his head with a deep, resigned sigh. "But you're right." He stood from his chair and straightened his coat. "We've no choice. Tell Danil to compile a list of his needs—his *needs*, mind you, not his wants—and I'll see if we can make him good, at least until he can get his first catch in."

Relief flooded through Julian, more than he thought it would. "Thank you, Master Mayor," he said, and Raedrick mirrored his words.

"Won't do much good though," Brimly said. "Not in the long run. Jakob was the brains of those two. If he doesn't recover..." He shook his head. "I'm not sure how long Danil can keep things solvent."

"Well," Raedrick said, carefully, "That's a problem we can deal with later, if it comes."

Brimly nodded. "Agreed." He leveled a hard look at the two of them. "In the meantime, you find that thief! I mean to hang him up by his fingernails in front of City Hall for a month!"

Julian tried to suppress a snort, but mostly failed. Brimly looked at him askance. "Something funny?"

"No, Master Mayor," he said, shaking his head quickly.

"Then get to it, gentlemen. And keep me informed. I want daily progress reports on this."

Son of a... That was going to be a major annoyance. He almost opened his mouth to object, but Raedrick beat him to it.

"Of course, Master Mayor." He gave a deep nod that was almost a half-bow, then he beckoned for Julian to follow and turned to leave the room.

❦ *9* ❦

# BRAINSTORM

"So what's the plan?"

Raedrick gave a little shrug of his shoulders and took a drink from his tankard. "The way I see it, there are only a few possibilities."

"Oh? I can think of dozens."

A long-suffering look was Raedrick's initial response. He raised one finger. "A disgruntled employee." A second finger. "Someone from the trading caravan."

Julian waited, but that was all Raedrick had to say. He snorted out a big exhalation.

They were back in The Oarlock for a late lunch of creamy noodles mixed with grilled fish, with a side of yesterday's bread. The crowd was not large, but certainly bigger than the taproom normally saw; the caravan men had not yet found the other establishments in town, or they simply preferred to remain in place. Either way, Molli could not be complaining.

He leaned forward. "Or Danil did it."

Raedrick raised an eyebrow.

"Seriously." Julian took a long swig of ale. "He's resentful that Jakob won't let him run the business the way he thinks it should be run. He's the older brother, you know. Older brother's

45

supposed to call the shots. But no, Jakob keeps running roughshod over everything. Finally, this morning, it becomes more than Danil can stand, and he snaps." He made a little punching gesture. "He smashes Jakob upside the head with a rock or something. Then he uses some of the tools in the warehouse to pry the safe door off and moves the money into his house. But when he comes back, the fishing men are beginning to clamor for their money, and worst of all, Jakob's not dead. So he panics and locks the door." He grinned at Raedrick. "Which is when I showed up."

Raedrick was silent for a long time, just looking at him. Finally, he began to laugh.

"What?"

Raedrick shook his head and wiped tears of mirth from his eyes. "That is the worst theory I've ever heard."

Julian snorted. "No worse than yours. A disgruntled employee. What, we're going to investigate all two hundred fifty of them?"

"If need be. But," he glanced around the taproom furtively for a second to make sure no one was close enough to hear, "I think it's more likely a caravan man. A local would not believe he could get away with it, because he has to stay here and how could he explain suddenly having all that money? Besides, everyone in town knows how vital the fishing company is here. I can't believe a local would do that to his neighbors."

Julian made a dismissive wave. "There are scum in every group, Rae. You know that. I can think of half a dozen men in town who I wouldn't put it past to sell out their own mothers if it came down to..." He trailed off as another thought came to him. Of course! "Come to think of it, you're right. It's not a local. But the caravan's not been here long enough to learn where and when to find the Covington Brothers' gold." He leaned forward and grinned triumphantly. "But we know a person who's not a local who has been."

Raedrick frowned thoughtfully for a moment. Then he blinked, his eyes widening. He got it.

"Let's get that little weasel."

Julian moved to stand, but Raedrick shot a hand across the table and grabbed his arm in a firm grip. He stared into Julian's eyes, his gaze hard as steel. "No, Julian. It wasn't Tolburt."

"No? Why not? He's just the type."

"No!"

Julian scowled at his friend. Why was he so blind when it came to Tolburt? Oh sure, Rae felt guilty about leaving him behind way back when. But that was more than made up for, and Tolburt had never shown himself to be anything but a sniveling, backbiting...

A clearing throat off to the right made Julian flinch before he caught himself. He turned to see who it was, and saw Marshall Leminster standing beside their table, a quizzical expression on his face.

"Gentlemen. You look like you're about to rip each others' heads off." His tone was mildly teasing, but his eyes told a different story. They were flinty, disapproving, as he looked them over.

Raedrick released Julian's arm and drew himself up. "Marshall," he said. "What can we do for you?"

Leminster looked between them once more, then gave a little shrug and said, "I actually came by to ask what *I* could do for *you*." He gestured toward the empty chair at their table. Raedrick nodded and, after a second, Julian did the same. Leminster sat quickly. "Heard what happened over at the fishing company," he said. "I imagine the whole town has. Thought maybe you could use some extra hands in the investigation."

"We were just talking about that," Raedrick said. "Comparing theories."

He glanced Julian's way, and Julian gave his shoulders a little roll and relaxed back in his seat. He let the irritation flow out of him, and forced himself to admit Raedrick was probably correct. Tolburt was just the guy to do this, but he was also pretty heavily controlled these days, between Holb as task master and Raedrick continually following up with him. And he was stuck in town, so he would have the same difficulty as anyone who was a local: what to do with the loot?

Julian sighed, then gave a full shrug. "We've settled on looking at people who don't live here. Which means the caravan." He grinned wickedly at Leminster. "Or you, I suppose. Where were you early this morning?"

Leminster looked askance at Julian, frowning. But after a couple seconds, his frown turned into a soft chuckle. "Asleep upstairs, that's where." He paused, considering. Then he gave a little nod of his head toward the back corner. "You'll want to talk with Alec Sarillo back there. Caravan's his baby."

Julian followed Leminster's nod to a small table in the back where three men sat, apparently deep in conversation. Two had their backs to him, so he couldn't make them out except to tell they were husky. The third was older, with hair that had been dark but was now so interspersed with grey that he almost looked like he had stripes. He was thin and sat stiffly erect, and dressed in the sort of finery that you didn't normally see in Lydelton.

"We'll make a point of it," Raedrick said, also looking that man over for a moment before turning back to Leminster. "It looked like there were a good twenty or thirty men in the caravan, all told?"

Leminster pursed his lips, then gave a quick nod.

"That's a lot of possibilities," Julian said. "Feel like doing some interviews?"

"Don't see why not. I'll have Job and Iven start asking some questions. They've been pretty friendly with some of the drivers, so that can't hurt." The Marshall scratched at his beard for a second. "But if you don't mind, I've got a better use for Bart."

"Oh?" Raedrick sounded intrigued.

"Well," Leminster put on an ingratiating smile. "Meaning no offense, but you two've never worked a case like this before have you?"

Julian shook his head.

Leminster made a quick nod, as though acknowledging something he knew would be the case. "Could be you missed something at the scene. These sorts of things... Well, there's an art to safecracking, and there are telltale signs that a man leaves. They can tell you what tools he used, and what techniques. That could help narrow the field a bit."

"You want to look at the crime scene," Raedrick said.

"More Bart than me. He's an expert on this sort of thing; it's what he worked down in the Capital. Ain't no one better to look around that scene than him, at least not in these parts."

Yeah, he certainly looked the type to be an expert, bland, and observant, as he was. He probably got all manner of criminals telling him secrets before they even knew they were doing it. Julian caught an inquiring glance from Raedrick and shrugged back at him. If Bart and Leminster could shed more light on what happened, why not?

"We'll be happy for your help, Marshall," Raedrick said.

Leminster nodded again and pushed himself up from the table. "Right. We'll get right to it, then." He lifted his finger to his brow in a quick salute. "Let you know what we find out." Then he turned on his heel and maneuvered through the tables toward the stairs at the back of the taproom. Off to fetch his men from upstairs, no doubt.

"Well, that ought to be helpful," Julian said, and shoveled the last forkful of lunch into his mouth. He almost didn't notice the succulent flavor as he considered the next move they needed to make. His eyes moved back to the caravan master in the back and he swallowed. "You want to go talk with Sarillo now or wait til later?"

Raedrick flashed a grin ever so briefly then pushed his plate away, despite half of his lunch still sitting there untouched. "No better time than the present."

Julian nodded and stood, gathering up his tankard as he did. Raedrick joined him, and they together set off to see what the fancy trading man had to say for himself.

‹❧  10  ❧›

# CARAVAN MASTER

From up close, Julian could see that the other two men at Sarillo's table were not as similar as he had thought from afar. Both were broad, but while the man on the right gained his girth from fat, the other was all muscle. They also dressed different. The muscular fellow wore simple brown woolens, and Julian saw the glint of mail beneath his outer layer. The other man was more colorful, boisterous even, and his clothing was loose-fitting. Maybe he thought that would help conceal his paunch.

As he and Raedrick approached the table, Sarillo noticed them and gave a little nod of his head in their direction, and the other two men turned to watch them. Muscle-man wore a very closely-trimmed brown beard to match his head, while the blubbery one was blond and clean-shaven. Both studied them closely as they approached.

"Good afternoon," Raedrick said, stopping a pace from the table. "Master Sarillo is it?"

Sarillo narrowed his eyes, focusing on the pins Julian and Raedrick wore on their left breasts. The badge of the town Constable was well known in these parts, a silver clenched fist holding a pair of scales, and he certainly would recognize it. After a few seconds' scrutiny, Sarillo smiled thinly at them.

"Constables. To what do I owe the pleasure?" His voice was strong, his tone refined, almost haughty, but Julian thought he detected an undercurrent of uncertainty there for some reason.

"I'm Raedrick Baletier." Raedrick gestured at Julian. "This is my partner, Julian Hinderbrook. We're investigating the robbery at the Covington Brothers' warehouse."

Sarillo frowned. "Terrible business, that. We were just discussing it. That event has the potential to ruin our entire prospects for this portion of our journey. Hasn't it Jerit?"

The plump man bobbed his head, looking if possible even more displeased than Sarillo.

Small wonder they were upset. From what Danil said, probably a substantial percentage of the goods they had brought for sale in the Vale were meant for the Covington Brothers. If that transaction failed to go through, it could possibly change the journey from profitable to extremely costly.

Which ruled Sarillo himself out as a suspect.

Raedrick glanced at Jerit for a second then looked back at Sarillo. "May we ask you a few questions?"

"Surely you don't think I'm involved?" Sarillo sounded affronted, but from the expression on his face Julian thought sure it was an act. He had to know why they had come over.

"Of course not," Julian said. "You're an honest businessman, I'm sure. But your men - "

The muscular man snorted. "None of my boys would go in for that." He grinned at them, a smile that advertised a love of physical violence, not of skulking. "Ain't their thing."

Sarillo chuckled ever so softly. "Cooper is my head of security," he said. "I daresay he knows the men better than I."

"In that case," Raedrick turned his gaze more fully upon Cooper, "do any of your boys have debts, Cooper? Family problems? Any reason they might be tempted - "

"Told you. My boys are solid. They ain't got nothing to do with it."

Which meant they *had* something to do with it. But right then, Julian didn't think Cooper would take kindly to his pointing out a double negative, so just this once he held his tongue.

Sarillo shook his head, his expression the very appearance of regretful. "I'm sorry we cannot be of more assistance, Constables. Now, if you will excuse us, we are very busy."

Their table was bare, with the exception of a nearly empty wineglass in front of Sarillo and tankards in front of Cooper and Jerit. They sure looked busy.

Julian exchanged a long look with Raedrick. His friend's lips were compressed in annoyance that Julian shared completely. But there was nothing else for it but to leave these fellows to their… whatever it was they were doing. He gave a little shrug.

Raedrick inclined his head politely in Sarillo's direction. "Thank you, gentlemen." He turned to go, but stopped halfway through his turn and looked back at the caravan master. "I must ask that you not leave town until we have completed our investigation."

Chagrin appeared on Jerit's face. He turned his gaze back toward Sarillo and opened his mouth to speak, but a raised hand from his boss stopped him.

"I'm afraid that's unacceptable Constable. We are on a tight timeline. If we do not make it through the pass to Calas before - "

Julian had had about enough of that. He leaned forward slightly from the hips and put on his best fierce soldier look. "You don't understand. That wasn't actually a request. Try to leave town before we give approval, and there will be trouble."

Cooper's eyes lit up—with eagerness?—and he licked his lips, looking first Julian and then Raedrick up and down, appraisingly. Then he smirked.

Sarillo's brow furrowed, his lips turning downward into a scowl. "Very well," he said, his tone so cold it was brittle. "We will remain. For a time." But only as long as I say we will, his tone and manner said. But that was probably the best they were going to get from him.

Raedrick returned the look with his best Squad Leader Who's Dressing Down A Dumb-Ass Private expression for a moment. Then he inclined his head again. "Good day, gentlemen."

Julian followed Raedrick as he left the vicinity of the caravan master's table. "That was..." he paused, searching for the right word.

"Less than helpful."

Julian nodded. "Makes a fellow wonder why he was so eager to be rid of us. Couldn't be that he's not nearly the honest businessman he wants everyone to think he is, could it?"

Raedrick paused to let a barmaid pass ahead of them, frowning. "It wouldn't surprise me if he turned out to be crooked in some way. But to be involved in the robbery?" He shook his head.

"Agreed. I just wonder what he *is* up to." There was a good chance they would never know.

Julian looked back over his shoulder at them before he followed Raedrick out of The Oarlock's front door, and saw Jerit staring after them. It was too far to tell for sure, but Julian thought the chubby fellow looked very troubled, indeed.

## TO CRACK A SAFE

Back at the Constabulary again. Julian took a moment to stoke the fire in the stove and add more fuel while Raedrick brought Geoff some water. They had spent a fruitless hour trying to talk to some of the caravan's wagon drivers as they were tending their horses in The Oarlock's stables. Bad enough they brought part of that smell back to the office with them, but they could at least have gotten something for their efforts.

The fresh wood popped, and a few sparks shot out of the open door at the front of the stove. Julian cursed softly and stamped out the embers as they landed on the floor, then shut the door with a soft clang. Then he removed his baldric and leaned it against the wall before flopping into his chair.

His brain ran in circles, going over the details of the case as they knew it and coming up completely empty. He realized he was scowling. Well, at least the thief, whoever he was, was still in town. That was something at least.

The door swung open, interrupting his musings with a blast of cold air, followed by Marshall Leminster. He gave a quick nod of greeting and pulled the door closed. Then he stomped his boots to kick off the slush from his soles.

"Constable," Leminster said. "Is your partner here?"

"In back," Julian said, gesturing toward the cell block door. He narrowed his eyes, looking Leminster over for a moment. He had a look of concern, or irritation, about him. "How's your day?"

Leminster gave a little shrug and started to reply. But right then Raedrick stepped back into the room from the cell block. Seeing the Marshall, Raedrick nodded in greeting, then turned to close and lock the door behind him.

"Ah good," Leminster said. "Bart has made some discoveries at your crime scene, and I really think you ought to come have a look."

"Happy to." Julian was on his feet and slipping his baldric over his shoulder in a flash. If Bart was the expert Leminster claimed, this should be interesting at the least. And it beat sitting here and stewing.

Raedrick looked at him with amusement for a second, then nodded agreement. "Let's go."

***

The warehouse office was much as they had left it, except that the blood on the floor had been cleaned up. The safe door still sat leaning against the wall as before, and as far as Julian could tell nothing else in the office had been moved. They had been explicit with Jakob about that: no one was to go into the office until they finished their investigation. And truth to tell, there was no reason *for* anyone to go there. With the lake frozen, there was nothing for the fishing company to do except pay the men each month and close the deal with Sarillo's caravan, and neither necessarily required them to use the office.

And now, with the money gone...

Bart was squatting next to the safe when they entered, his lips pursed in contemplation. It took him a moment to notice their entrance, which surprised Julian. As closely as Bart always seemed to study his surroundings, he would not have thought the Marshall would miss a fly hovering from across the room.

"Cap," Bart said to Leminster when he saw them, coming to his feet smoothly. His movements reminded Julian of a dancer's, they were so fluid.

Leminster nodded greeting to his man, then gestured toward Julian and Raedrick. "Tell them what you told me please, Bart."

Bart turned to regard the pair of them, his features perplexed. "Constables," he said. "I've seen a lot of safe-cracking jobs in my time, but I'm not sure I've ever seen one quite like this."

It was remarkable. These were among the first words Julian could recall hearing Bart speak. Given how unobtrusive the rest of his persona was, Julian would have figured Bart's voice would be soft, bland, easy to miss. On the contrary, he spoke with quiet confidence. And his tone... It was almost melodious, and Julian found himself perking up a little and paying close attention, from the pleasure of hearing those tones if for nothing else.

Bart probably had a tremendous singing voice.

Raedrick did not seem as impressed as Julian was. "What do you mean? How many ways are there to get a safe open?"

Bart snorted softly. "Literally dozens. Each safe build has a different design, and will require a different technique to get it open." He pointed toward the lone window in the office. "The lock on that window was forced; that's how they got in. Nothing unusual about that. But look here." He gestured for them to come over and squatted back down in front of the broken safe.

Julian and Raedrick complied, squatting next to him as he continued speaking.

"This safe is a Terrayn Sixteen-Fifty, among the best safes you can get for medium loads. Very difficult to crack. Impossible unless you've studied them and practiced extensively."

Julian had seen that safe before the robbery. From the look of it, he would have said it was impossible to get into, no matter what. Clearly not. "Could *you* get it open?"

Bart shot him a glance that contained part surprise and part amusement. "I've tried my hand at them before. Best way to catch a thief is to know how he plies his trade."

"I take it that's a no."

Bart's brow furrowed, his initial amusement becoming irritation.

Raedrick stepped in quickly. "So the thief knows what he's doing. He's probably done this sort of thing several times before." He frowned, chewing on his lips slightly. "How did he get it open?"

Bart looked back at the safe and also frowned. "That is the puzzling part. He took the door off its hinges, which is not strictly speaking necessary, and really will do you no good unless you can also disable the locking mechanism itself. But I don't see any scratches or scoring in the metal. The sort of heavy tools you'd have to use to pull the door off like that would leave marks."

"Ok," Julian began.

"And look here," Bart said, leaning closer in and pointing to the top and bottom of the opening where the safe's door used to rest.

Julian peered closer. On both sides of the opening, there was a small circular darkening of the metal, like someone had rubbed charcoal on it. But when he touched it, the discoloration did not rub off. He looked back at Bart, quizzically.

"That," Bart said, "is where the locking bars slide into place. Or at least that's what should be there. Look here at the door." He pointed at the top of the door. On the back side, as he said, there were two bars on pivots that looked like they would slide into place. But looking at them, they were slightly warped and had that same discoloration at their tips. "Those bars are supposed to extend farther than the door, into the holes in the safe's body. But they've been cut short."

"What do you mean, cut short?" Raedrick asked. His brow was deeply furrowed as he tried to put the pieces together. Julian was having similar difficulty.

"I mean, it looks like the locking bars were somehow sliced

through. If you feel where the holes in the safe body should be, you can just feel where the body's metal ends and the bars begin."

"But..." Julian began. Then he stopped, baffled. "What could do that?"

Bart shook his head. "I have no idea. I've never see a tool that could do this, or remove the door entirely, not without leaving a mark." He rose, wiping his hands together and frowning. "It's a complete mystery."

"Like it happened by magic."

Bart narrowed his eyes and looked at Raedrick, considering for a moment. Then he shrugged slightly. "That's as good an explanation as any."

Julian and Raedrick traded long looks. Julian racked his brain but could not come to a different conclusion. A person cracked this safe using methods and tools that the Marshall's safe expert could neither identify nor explain. Cut off the locking bars somehow, without leaving a mark.

He got that familiar sinking feeling in his stomach, and had to suppress a groan. The gods could not hate them enough to send another rogue mage through their little town again.

Could they?

## OF ITEMS MAGICAL

Leminster and Bart parted ways with them as they all left the warehouse, the two Marshalls turning toward the side street that led over to The Oarlock. Julian watched them wade through the slowly growing slush piles as the waning day, warmer than it had been in a week or more despite its chill, slowly diminished the snowdrifts. He was in dire need of a drink. He did *not* want to get involved with magical chicanery again, not after what happened last summer when the mad mage Telurian brought his Out-Dweller into their midst.

But if wishes could accomplish anything, he would be richer than the king, with his own private harem to go along with the money. He sighed. "Guess we'd better talk to Melanie."

Raedrick frowned thoughtfully. "I'm not sure I want to involve her. If Leminster and his men find out about her..." He left the rest unsaid.

"I think that cat's left the bag, Rae. Loran Haversted's told the Magestirium about her months ago."

Raedrick paused for a long several seconds, then blew out a sigh of resignation. "You're right, no doubt. And even if you're not, we have little choice." He turned toward Main Street, and Julian followed him.

A walk of about ten minutes found them outside the door to Melanie's shop. Raedrick hesitated for a moment before taking hold of the latch, as though steeling himself. Then he grasped the latch resolutely and swung the door open, to the tinkling of Melanie's little bell.

A different incense was burning than when Julian had been there earlier. This one was sharper, almost tangy, the way an orange bites against the tongue. But it was pleasant, nonetheless, and Julian felt his spirits rise, some of the tension he had been holding fading away as he breathed its aroma.

The shop was empty, not unexpected as most people were done with business for the day and were settling in at home, or soon would be. Melanie sat alone on her stool behind the counter, peering intently at a book, one of the books she had received from the caravan unless Julian missed his guess. She glanced up as they entered and crooked an eyebrow at them.

"Well," she said wryly, "this can't be good."

Julian snorted softly. "What? We can't both pay a visit if we want to?"

Melanie inserted a place mark and closed the book's cover with a soft thump. "The last time the two of you came in here looking like that we nearly got killed by an Out-Dweller." She shook her head, not looking at all amused. "What fire do you need me to pull you out of this time?"

You had to hand it to her, she certainly could see through to the center of things when she wanted to. Julian glanced at Raedrick, who gave a little shrug as if to say, "This is your horse, partner."

"Well," Julian said, turning back to Melanie, "looks like that robbery is more complicated than we thought it was."

"I'm not surprised," she said, and the irony practically dripped from her words. "Do tell."

"Do you know of a way to cut through metal without leaving any marks?"

Both eyebrows rose, and her eyes widened. "Give me the details."

It only took a couple minutes to share what Bart had discovered, and by the time Julian finished, Melanie's lips were pursed and she was tapping at them with her index finger as she stared into space, thoughtfully. She remained quiet for some time.

Finally, after an interminable silence, Raedrick cleared his throat. "Melanie."

She gave a little jerk, then looked back at them with chagrin, and a hint of embarrassment. "I was thinking of something Timon once told me." At the mention of her dead lover's name, Julian thought he saw a hint of...something...in her eyes. Pain, he assumed, but it fled as quickly as it came. "I had just managed to cast a simple fire spell. He had made me work at it all afternoon, and I was deathly tired. I also felt like I should have mastered it sooner, and the flame I made was pathetically small. He smiled and tried to encourage me to keep practicing by saying when I had truly mastered it, I would be able to make a flame so concentrated, so hot, that I could burn through a metal bar like a razor cutting through paper." She smirked. "That was not as encouraging as he hoped it would be. I made him find a different way later on." The smirk turned into a sly, secretive grin.

Raedrick looked away and, to Julian's amusement, flushed slightly. For his part, Julian found he could go right on listening to Melanie talk about that sort of thing if she had a care to. But, alas, it had nothing to do with their current puzzle.

"So our culprit is definitely a mage then," he said, rather proud of himself for keeping a straight face and a serious, professional tone.

Melanie's grin faded, and she looked back at him and shook her head. "Not necessarily."

"But you just said - "

She held up a hand to forestall his sentence. "I know what I said. It certainly *could* be a mage, but anyone who is advanced enough to make a flame like that has had years of training and experience, and stands fairly high in the Magestirium. Those are not the sorts of men who need to break into penny-ante businesses in a flyspeck of a village in the middle of nowhere."

Julian recalled when they first met, and how she had...accurately...described Lydelton thus. He had agreed at the time, despite finding the place charming, but now he was startled to find offense welling up within him at her words. She had no call to talk about his—about their—town like that. He realized he was scowling at the same time Melanie's eyebrow rose.

"Really, Julian. I call this place home now, too, but I've no illusions about its relevance in the world."

Why, she... Hang it all, she was right. Still, it irked him to hear her say it like that.

Funny the difference a year makes.

Raedrick jumped in then. "You could have said the same thing about members of the Magestirium going mad and becoming enthralled by Out-Dwellers, but we all know what happened with Telurian last summer. And don't forget the mage who was teamed up with Isenholf."

Melanie paused, then inclined her head, conceding the point. "True. But I think it's safe to say Telurian was a special case, and the other man..." She shrugged. "He was of middling skill."

"I seem to recall *you* having some trouble with him."

Melanie's eyes narrowed. "By that, I mean he did not stand high in the ranks of the Magestirium. If he had been, he would have had no incentive to become a bandit, as much wealth as the Magestirium commands."

Julian snorted. "I'm heard of all manner of *noblemen* turning to crime. It's not always a matter of money."

Melanie threw up her hands in annoyance. "We could argue this all day. But you're missing my point."

Raedrick cast an annoyed look Julian's way, and he returned it with one of his own. Was she being *deliberately* obtuse?

"What *is* your point, Melanie?" Raedrick asked, levelly.

She rolled her eyes, clearly as annoyed as both he and

Raedrick felt. "My point is it did not have to be a mage." She looked between the two of them and no doubt saw the utter confusion Julian felt because she rolled her eyes again. "Do you recall the trigger to the Trans-planar Rift that I found on Isenholf's mage?"

Julian blinked, the sudden change in subject leaving him even more confused. He had not thought about that bit of...obsidian she called it...in nearly a year. He looked at Raedrick, who was nodding as though he totally understood where she was going with this.

"I do. Did you ever figure out how to make it work?"

Melanie's brow furrowed, and if anything she looked even more annoyed. "No. The thing is a mystery wrapped up in an enigma." She shook her head, as though to clear her thoughts. "But that's not relevant right now." She held up and index finger. "What *is* relevant is that trigger has within it the magical capacity to open the Trans-planar Rift, if one knows how to activate it. Other objects can be crafted that contain the energies of other spells as well."

Julian blinked. "They can?"

She gave him a long-suffering look. "Such objects are exceptionally difficult—and expensive—to construct, and thus are extremely rare. But they can be used by just about anyone, provided the person is shown the method of their activation."

"I don't imagine these things are just left lying around," Raedrick mused.

Melanie shook her head. "The Magestirium has a number of vaults where they keep such items. Practitioners who make them, or find them out in the world, are under strict orders to return them there for safe keeping." She pursed her lips. "Timon told me the penalty for not doing so is...severe."

"So only the Magestirium can make them, and the only place they're stored is in their vaults," Julian said.

Melanie nodded.

"How does that mean our suspect doesn't have to be a mage?"

"Because not all of the magical constructs that have ever been created have been found and returned there. And - "

"And because not everyone in the Magestirium is scrupulous. Some may find them and keep them for themselves, or sell them for a tidy profit." Raedrick said, completing her thought for her.

Melanie nodded agreement. "It would have to be a construct that has not been turned in, though. Timon said they keep tight control over the items in their vaults, and perform regular inventories. Taking an item out of the Magestirium would be nigh-on impossible, and even if it were done, the theft would be discovered quickly. Few would be foolish enough to even attempt it."

Julian frowned, turning that over in his mind for a moment. "So either we've got another mage running around or someone has one of those constructs. And the most likely place to get one of those constructs is from a member of the Magestirium, who are based in the Capital. So..."

"Definitely not a local," Raedrick said, sounding imminently satisfied with himself. He gave Julian a beatific smile that only served to irritate him all the more—Raedrick's very intention, no doubt.

Julian raised his hands in surrender. "Ok, I'm convinced. But that doesn't leave us any closer to figuring out who our thief is. It's still got to be someone in that caravan."

"Sure it does," Raedrick said. "How many of those drivers and guards were locals from Mangin City that Sarillo hired for this trip? I'll bet far fewer than half have ever been anywhere near the Capital. And besides," he glanced at Melanie, "these things are expensive; not just anyone could afford one."

Melanie nodded agreement.

"Who says he bought it?" Julian said.

Raedrick gave him a long-suffering look, but after a moment, he was forced to nod, conceding the point.

They just looked at each other for a long moment. Finally, Raedrick looked back at Melanie. "Is there any way to detect these constructs?"

She frowned in thought for a few seconds, then shrugged. "There may be, but I don't know off-hand. I have some of Timon's notes that I managed to save when the Inquisitors took him. I can look to see if they have any more information."

"Please do," Raedrick said. He looked back at Julian. "In the meantime, we'll have to rely on interviews."

Julian sighed, but nodded agreement. "My favorite thing."

He turned toward the door, and Raedrick followed. He had just grasped the latch when Melanie called from behind, "You're welcome."

Julian turned back around and gave her an abashed smile. "Sorry." Then a thought came to him and he made his smile bigger. He swept into his deepest, most courtly bow. "You have our eternal gratitude, fair lady. I don't know how we can ever think to repay you."

She just looked at him crossly for a few seconds, then she burst out laughing. She shook her head and made a dismissive wave at them, then turned and swept through the beaded doorway into her back room, still laughing in amusement.

## ❦ 13 ❦

## A QUIET CHAT

The last sliver of the sun's disk was visible above the mountains to the east when they emerged from Melanie's shop, and the shadows had grown long. Twilight, short-lived as it was in the Vale, was creeping over the land. Down the street a ways, a member of the Lamplighters' Guild, bundled up against the swiftly deepening cold as evening settled upon them, was about his duties.

Julian flipped the cowl of his cloak up and pulled the rest of it about his body, too late to retain the warmth he had carried with him from inside. "Won't get much in the way of interviews done tonight, I don't think."

Raedrick looked like he was going to be stubborn about it for a minute, then he nodded agreement. "It's time to fetch Geoff's dinner from The Oarlock anyway."

"Might as well get some for ourselves as well."

Raedrick nodded agreement quickly, and they set off.

The mud of the side-streets clung to their boots, making squishing noises with each step, but Julian reflected it could be much worse. At least it wasn't ice anymore. All the same, by the time they reached the Inn, his feet felt like they weighed four times what they should have, and it took a full two minutes of determined scraping at Molli's doorstep to get enough of the mud off before he felt alright about setting foot inside her place.

The taproom was bustling, and no wonder. Off to the left, Helen MacAllef and two of her friends had set up on a stage that Mollie assembled a couple nights a week. Between Helen's voice, Kari's harp, and Ysolde's drum, they always put on a fine performance, and it looked as though tonight was going to be no different. A good-sized bunch had crowded into all of the tables in their vicinity, and a number of people stood nearby as well. Julian noted that many of the faces belonged to the caravan drivers, and several of the guards, in addition to the regular townsfolk.

They might be able to learn a thing or two tonight, after all.

But first, dinner.

He and Raedrick threaded their way through the crowd and found a table in the rear, near the stairs leading up to the lodging rooms, and settled down. A young blonde barmaid—Tami if Julian remembered correctly, and he usually did—hurried up to them, smiling a bright smile of greeting above her apron and working dress.

"Two ales," Julian said, "and whatever Molli's got prepared for dinner."

Tami beamed another smile at them and nodded, then hurried away toward the bar, where as usual, Molli held court, along with Rolf.

Julian looked around, and was surprised at Lani's absence. "Lani not working tonight?"

Raedrick gave a little shake of his head. "She's ill."

Julian blinked in surprise. "She looked fine yesterday."

An eyebrow rose on Raedrick's forehead. "Well, this morning she couldn't keep her breakfast down." He shrugged. "Probably the weather changing. I expect she'll be better in a day or..."

He trailed off as movement from the right drew his eye, and his eyes widened in surprise. Julian turned to look, and saw Lani descending the stairs from above. She wore a blue dress and a white apron, and had her blonde hair tied up in a bun atop her head. She wore a frown, but when she saw the two of them that fled, replaced by a warm, cheery smile.

She walked over and, upon reaching the table, bent over and gave Raedrick a light kiss on the cheek. "Good evening," she said softly as she straightened. Then she turned toward Julian. "Good to see you, Julian," she said, resting her hand on Raedrick's shoulder and giving it a light squeeze.

"Uh," Julian said, "you too, Lani." He glanced between her and Raedrick, then added, lamely, "You look like you're feeling better."

Lani gave him a baffled look.

Raedrick cleared his throat. "You were sick this morning."

"Oh." She made a dismissive wave of her hand. "That passed soon enough. A bad bit of fish, I expect."

Or too much ale last night, Julian didn't say.

"You boys been taken care of yet?"

Julian nodded quickly. "Tami got us."

"Good." She gave Raedrick's shoulder another squeeze. "I've got to go talk with mother." Her lips twisted into a grimace. "*Master* Sarillo has more complaints about his lodgings." She shook her head in disgust.

Julian winced. That fellow did seem as though he would be the complaining type.

Raedrick frowned. "Has he given you much trouble?"

She shrugged. "No more than he ever does. Problem is, each time he comes through he's got a different set of issues. If it were consistent, that would be one thing, but..." She let the rest go unsaid, the consternation in her voice doing the speaking for her. She drew a breath, then forced a smile back onto her face. "Anyway, I'd better get his latest needs seen to, or we'll never hear the end of it." She looked down at Raedrick and her smile turned more warm. "See you later?"

Raedrick nodded, returning the smile with one that dripped even more sappiness. Julian almost gagged.

Lani departed, heading over to where Molli held court. Raedrick followed her with his eyes as she went.

Julian turned to look at her as well for a moment, then turned back to Raedrick and gave him a teasing grin. "You planning to make an honest woman out of her, or are you going to keep leading her on forever?"

Raedrick's brows shot up for a second, then they furrowed and he gave Julian a flat look.

"What? Everyone in town's wondering. Figured I would be the one to ask."

"Is that right," he said flatly.

Julian nodded. "Well, truth be told, Horace told me that if I didn't get you moving, he was going to send some of his boys to thump some sense into you."

Raedrick's expression soured even further. Julian wasn't sure, but he thought he saw steam leaking from his ears.

Tami returned just then, carrying a tray with two foaming tankards atop and beaming her bright smile at them. "Here you go, Constables," she said in an alto that sounded like it would always just miss the correct note. It made a jarring combination with her otherwise pleasant demeanor.

"Thanks, Tami," Julian said as she placed his tankard in front of him, and she gave him a little wink.

He paused in the act of reaching for his drink, the unexpected flirtation setting him aback for a second.

Tami set Raedrick's tankard down and turned away, her hips making a little sashay as she swept past Julian toward the bar. He turned around to watch her go, bemusement and surprise fighting a little battle within his head.

He turned back around to find Raedrick gazing at him with a cocked eyebrow. "Something I should know about, there?" he asked, making a little nod in Tami's direction.

Julian shrugged and picked up his tankard. He drank deeply, then wiped the foam from his lips with the back of his hand as he replaced the tankard on the table. "Dunno. She's pretty enough, I suppose, but we've never..." He looked back over his shoulder and shrugged again. "Too young for me, anyway."

Raedrick snorted out a laugh as he took a drink. "When has that ever stopped you?"

That earned him a scowl in return. "Don't think I don't see what you're doing. You're not getting off the hook that easily, my friend." Julian shook a finger at him.

Raedrick sighed and set his tankard back on the table, and stared into it. He was silent for a long several seconds. "I don't know." He took a long breath. "I'm not sure what to do, to be honest."

Julian snorted. "It's not that difficult, Rae. Do you love the girl?"

Raedrick blinked. "What?"

Now he was just being obtuse. Seriously, first Melanie and now him? If people kept this up, Julian was going to have to hit someone tonight. He just looked at his former squad leader levelly. After a moment, Raedrick flushed, and shrugged.

"I don't know. I think so? But - "

"You think so?" Julian rolled his eyes. "Sounds to me like you don't."

"What do you - "

"If you have to spend hours asking yourself if you love some-one, you don't love them. Or at least, you don't *love them*, love them. If you know what I mean."

Raedrick frowned, and all of a sudden his face was a mask of indecision and confusion. "But that's just it, Julian. I do, but…"

He trailed off as Tami returned, this time with two plates on her tray, from which wisps of steam rose, carrying the scents of hot spices and pork.

Not fish? This was a rare treat, from Molli's kitchen.

Tami set the plates down with another smile, then went back about her rounds. Julian dug in.

It was just as delicious as the aroma led him to believe. The spices put a pleasant burn on his tongue, and the meat was cooked to that perfect point that was not too well done so that it still retained its juice. And the bread was so soft he could have sworn the cooks had just pulled it from the oven special for them.

Sopping up some of the juices with a hunk of that bread, he looked back up at Raedrick. "Well?"

Raedrick finished chewing and swallowed, a thoughtful frown on his face. "I hear what you're saying, but it's not as simple as - "

A sudden ruckus from the front of the taproom interrupted and drew both their eyes.

A group of men in the grey cloaks the Fishing Guild preferred to wear stood in the gap between the cluster of tables in front of the stage and the bar, facing off against a like number of men who Julian recognized as wagon drivers from the caravan. Behind them, several of the guards watched, ugly expressions on their faces.

And in the center between the two groups, two fellows—one of the fishing men and one of the drivers—wrestled on the ground, looking for all the world like they were trying to rip each others' eyes out.

Julian took the scene in at a glance, and then groaned as his stomach sank. This was all they needed.

## ❧  14  ❧

## BAR BRAWL

Julian left his chair and elbowed his way across the room toward the tussling men, nearly running poor Tami over as he went. She had to leap backward to get out of his way, and the look she gave him as he stormed past held none of the playful flirtation she had been showing before.

More people were moving toward the fight, slowly forming a ring around the combatants, and Julian had to shove his way through to reach the scene of the duel. There he stopped for a moment to take stock.

The driver was on top of the Fishing Man—from up close now, Julian could see it was Worly, one of the newer hands on the boats —and had his hands latched around the prone fellow's throat. For his part, Worly was also choking the driver, but that couldn't last, not with leverage against him. Both men were making grunting noises, while on all sides the onlookers were adding their voices to the fray.

"Choke 'im out, Farley!"

"Get up, Worly!"

"Beat him into mush!"

Farley—Julian presumed that was the driver—seemed to take that last as great advice, because he released Worly's throat his his right hand and raised it up above his head, his fingers curling into a fist.

That was about enough of that. Julian lunged forward, and grabbing hold of that raised hand with his right, cupped his left hand around the front of Farley's face. A quick twist of his hips had the wagon driver off of Worly and falling onto the floor to the side.

"All right, that's enough!" Raedrick shouted in his best parade ground voice. He stood at the edge of the ring of men, his hands on his hips and his cloak thrown back so all could see his silver badge of office, and he gazed about with a stare that would freeze molten steel on contact.

Immediately the townsfolk quieted down. Several backed up a step, suddenly looking like they had somewhere else they really needed to be. Not the Fishing Men, though. They shut their traps, but they continued staring daggers at the caravan men opposite them.

For their part, the caravan men took a look at Raedrick and Julian, and if anything their scowls grew deeper. Before they could say anything, Raedrick turned his withering glare back on them. It looked like they collectively swallowed, but their scowls remained.

Julian walked over to Farley, who had begun to rise, and placed a boot onto his back, between his shoulder blades. "Don't move." Then he glanced back at Worly and scowled at him. "You either." He had to stop himself from spitting in disgust. "What are you two thinking, fighting in here?" Shaking his head, he looked back at Raedrick. "Nothing a night in the lockup won't cure, I expect."

Raedrick nodded agreement. "Worly." He looked quizzically at Farley. "Farley, is it?" Beneath Julian's boot, the driver nodded. "You're both under arrest."

"They started it, Constable!" one of the Fishing Men, who had been standing in the back of their little group, Julian noticed, said, a note of complaint in his voice.

"Bollocks," said a burly caravaner who looked thoroughly wicked with his bushy brown beard and a scar that ran halfway down his left cheek. "Your man there tackled Farley to the ground from out of nowhere."

"Nowhere? You stole our pay, you bastards!"

Ah hell. If the Fishing Men had gotten it into their heads that the caravaners were truly the cause of the robbery…

"The devil you say!"

And then the burly man charged across the floor toward the fishing men.

Or he would have, except Raedrick leapt in front of him, sword drawn. "Enough!" he roared, and the caravaner slid to a halt, his expression suddenly fearful and his hands raised to show his newly peaceful intentions. Raedrick scowled at him, then turned a slow circle, pointing his curved blade's point at every man present in turn. "I don't care *who* started it. Back off. Now. Any of you who are still in this room in ten seconds will join these two in jail."

All around, men glanced at each other, uncertainly. But no one made to leave.

Julian ground his teeth, then drew his own sword. "Move!" he shouted.

Apparently one bared blade was not enough to disperse them, but two did the trick. In moments, the Fishing Men and caravaners both cleared out, leaving only the townsfolk who had not been participating, Helen and her friends on the stage, and Molli and her taproom staff. And the two ruffians.

Raedrick swore under his breath and put his sword up. Then he cast an apologetic look in Molli's direction. "Looks like we ran off a good chunk of your clientele. Sorry about that."

Molli sniffed. "I'm just happy it stopped before anything got broken."

Or someone got hurt, she didn't say. And Julian couldn't say he blamed her for that one. Two fools hurting each other got what they deserved. Didn't mean they got to trash someone else's property, though.

"Alright," Julian said, looking down at the caravaner beneath his boot as he slid his sword back into his scabbard. "You're not going to give us any more trouble are you? Because right now I would love for you to try."

Farley turned his head to look up at him from the corner of his eye. The look on Julian's face must have convinced him he meant business, because Farley blanched and shook his head quickly. "N- No, sir," he said in a quavering voice.

"Good." Julian removed his foot and, bending over, grabbed Farley by his shoulders. "On your feet." The caravaner obeyed, meekly, for a wonder.

For his part, Morly offered no resistance. He just hung his head, looking as though he were suddenly reconsidering every poor decision he had ever made in his life. Raedrick stood next to him, holding onto the Fishing Man's right arm with his left hand. He looked Julian and Farley over briefly, then cast his gaze back Molli's way.

"Would you please send over dinner for our other prisoner, and send someone to fetch Horace and have him meet us at the Constabulary?"

Molli nodded, her face a mask of calm. But if Julian knew her at all, she was a raging inferno of fury inside, and woe to the barmaid or scullion who set a foot wrong for the rest of the night.

Raedrick returned the nod with an apologetic smile, then turned back to Julian. "Let's go."

"Hold on, Constable."

The voice issued from the rear of the taproom. Julian recognized it at once. Despite only hearing Cooper, the caravan security man, speak that once, he had a distinctive drawl.

They turned, and saw Cooper just stepping off the bottommost stair. He sauntered toward them, his thumbs hooked behind his sword belt. He was chewing on something that made his left cheek bulge outward. "That's my man there," he said. "Let 'im go."

Julian snorted. Loudly.

Raedrick gave Cooper a flat look. "You need to turn around and go back upstairs. Right now."

Cooper spat the thing he was chewing—it was a wad of some sort of vegetable—out onto the floor. From the corner of his eye, Julian saw Molli's eyes bulge, and suddenly that internal fury was completely visible. He was certain if she had been holding her usual wooden spoon she would have beaten Cooper within an inch of his life right that second.

"My man." Cooper said it as though that was all that needed to be said, as though that took primacy over everything.

Raedrick was having none of it. "My town. Here, brawlers spend the night in jail."

"If you have a problem with that," Julian added, silently hoping Cooper decided to press the issue, "you can join him there."

The security man scowled darkly, turning a gaze on them that promised some of that violence his earlier grin said he enjoyed.

They stood, staring at each other in silence for a long several moments. Farley began to tremble in Julian's grasp, and Julian could not help wonder whether he was more afraid that they would all throw down right there or that he and Raedrick would turn him over to Cooper.

Come to think on it, that might be a better punishment. But Cooper didn't get to decide justice here.

Finally, Cooper snorted. "Could be you'll come to regret that, Constable." Then, apparently deciding discretion was in fact the better part of valor, he said, "See you in the morning," to Farley in a tone that promised all manner of discomfort to follow. Then he turned on his heel and strode back to the staircase.

※ 15 ※

## CLEANUP

"**W**hat the hell was that?"

Julian shoved Farley into the cell that Raedrick held open, the one directly across from Geoff, and the caravan man stumbled inside, almost tripped over the leavings bucket before he got his balance. Raedrick shut the door and locked it, then shrugged in response to Julian's question with a scowl.

"On what plane of existence does a caravan security guy think he has authority over a Constable?"

Raedrick shrugged again, and moved over to the rearmost cell on the right, which he opened to allow the meek Worly to walk into. After the Fishing Man got settled, Raedrick locked up and turned back to Julian. "I don't know, Julian. He's certainly got an inflated sense of himself."

From his cell, Farley said in a quavering voice, "You don't want to go making him mad, Constables." His eyes darted about fearfully. "You really don't."

Julian snorted derisively. "Shut up."

He followed Raedrick out into the front office, then shut the cell block door behind them and stomped over to his desk. "Cooper. What an idiot. He's probably dead already. Molli prob-

81

ably clawed his eyes out and flayed him, and good riddance, too." He sat down in his chair and blew out a long exhalation. "That aside, this could be really bad, Rae, you know that. If Horace's boys decide to go after the caravan..." He left the rest unsaid.

Raedrick nodded solemnly as he sat down behind his own desk. "I'm hoping Horace will set them straight."

"After that stunt he pulled at the warehouse..." Julian shook his head, baffled. "Has everyone lost their minds this week? First that, then this brawl, then Cooper, then you and Lani - "

Raedrick scowled at him. Julian just gave him a level look in return. After a moment, Raedrick lowered his eyes.

"I know. You're right, ok?"

Julian blinked. That was not exactly expected. "About which part?"

Raedrick just looked at him. After a moment, Julian grinned. "Just remember that next time you start doubting me."

Raedrick snorted. Loudly.

A few minutes later, a knock at the door presaged Tami's arrival. Julian didn't expect her to be the one who delivered Geoff's food. Normally either Lani did it herself or Molli sent one of the stablehands. But then, normally he and Raedrick did not run off half of her customers for the night, and all the barmaids were busy.

"Constables," the barmaid said in her slightly out of tune voice. "I've got your food."

"Thanks Tami," Julian said, then he looked over at Raedrick. "Flip you for the duty?"

Raedrick chuckled, but instead of taking Julian up on the offer he stood and walked around his desk. "I'll take care of it." He accepted the bundled meal from Tami with a polite nod, then grabbed up the cell block key and headed back to give it to Geoff.

Tami watched him go, then turned a bright smile Julian's way. "You were brave tonight," she said.

He blinked in surprise. That was not exactly something that required bravery. Facing down forty-five bandits, just him and

Raedrick? Yup. Taking on a renegade mage with his own pet Out-Dweller? Definitely. But breaking up a barroom brawl? Where had she been the last year? Or had she not been paying attention at all?

"It was nothing," he said, trying to keep the amazement out of his voice. "Seen a dozen silly fights just like that."

Tami looked doubtful about something. But all she said was, "I'd better get back. Good evening, Constable."

"You too."

He watched her go, and shook his head when the door shut behind her. It was amazing what impressed some women.

Raedrick came back a moment later and shut the cell block door behind himself. "As soon as Horace gets here, we should go talk with the Mayor."

Julian shrank back from that thought. Not that he disliked the Mayor. He was a decent enough fellow. But he could be…flighty. Still, Raedrick was right. "Yeah, he may have to step in if Horace can't get his boys under control. And someone needs to give that Sarillo a talking to."

Raedrick nodded agreement. "Maybe he'll pay the Mayor more heed than he does us."

Somehow Julian doubted that.

---

As they waited for someone to answer Raedrick's knock, Julian realized that he had never before seen the inside of the Mayor's house. He certainly had a nice enough location, down Lake Road a few hundred yards past the western-most of Lydelton's finger piers. The Mayor's place backed right up to the lake, and probably commanded one hell of a view out his rear windows.

It was certainly large enough, too. Two stories and half again as wide as Melanie's shop. The Mayor had apparently been a very successful businessman before he hung up his commercial robes in favor of politics.

Not a bad deal, apparently.

It was full dark, and the temperature had dropped enough that the mud in the streets had begun to harden into dirty ice sheets. By the time they reached the house, Julian found himself chilled to the bone. And now, without brisk movement to help offset it, the cold seemed all the more bitter. He pulled his cloak tight as the seconds stretched and tried hard not to resent having to wait.

The door opened a crack and a middle-aged woman with greying hair that was done up in tight curls peered around the edge at them. She took them in at a glance, and the severe expression she wore on her face faded immediately.

"Oh, hello Constables," she said. "And Horace as well. My!" She swung the door open fully and stepped back, showing that she was wearing a thick pink and white robe over her ample girth. "Come in, please."

"Thank you, Mistress Brimly," Raedrick said politely.

Julian echoed him, and Horace knuckled his brow. The three of them kicked the mud and slush off their boots before entering.

Mistress Brimly shut the door behind them, and Julian had to force himself not to breathe a sigh of relief. The inside of the house was warm to the edge of roasting, and no wonder. The entryway deposited them into a large room that took up most of the first floor, and Julian saw three wood stoves in various locations around the room's circumference. A dining table and chairs sat off to the left, and bookshelves lined the wall to the right. A quartet of chairs with thick cushions surrounded a smaller table directly ahead, near a broad set of double doors that led out back to the lake and a wide window that offered a view of the same.

"Wil's upstairs, gentlemen," Mistress Brimly said. "I'll go get him."

She bustled off through a doorway that stood between two of the bookcases, and Julian let out a low whistle.

"Wow. I knew the Mayor had done well for himself, but I didn't realize..."

Horace nodded. "Most folks think the Covington brothers are the big money in town, but they forget that Brimly used to corner the market until about ten years ago." He shrugged slightly, then said more softly, "Some days I wonder if we wouldn't have been better off if..." He trailed off as the sound of heavy footsteps issued through the doorway Mistress Brimly had just disappeared through.

A second later, Mayor Brimly strode into the room. Unlike his wife, he was still dressed for the day, but he had removed his customary coat and was just in his shirtsleeves. He carried a glass that contained an amber fluid of some sort in his left hand, and when he saw them he gave them a look that said he really would have preferred to have been left in peace.

"Good evening, gentlemen," he said, and that look faded completely, replaced by a businesslike manner that carried through to his voice.

"Master Mayor," Raedrick said politely. "Some things have happened that you need to know about."

Brimly sipped at his glass and nodded. He gave a little sigh. "I expect I won't like hearing them, will I?"

Julian shook his head.

Brimly sighed more loudly. "In that case, we'd all better have a drink."

# 16

# MAYORAL ESTATE

I t was good to have money.

Julian had always known that, but just then, sitting in the Mayor's marvelously cushioned chair and sipping on whiskey that tasted as though it had been milked strait from the teat of the sex-goddess herself, he realized just how little he had truly appreciated that before.

He should have listened to his mother and gone into business, not joined the Army.

Oh well.

Across the small table from him, Brimly took a deep swallow of his whiskey and sank back into his chair. "Sarillo." He said the name like a curse. "I remember when he got his start. He was a snake then, and he's only gotten worse as the years went by."

Julian raised an eyebrow. "So he *is* crooked."

Brimly snorted. "Does the Healers Circle wear white?"

To his left, Raedrick scowled in disapproval. "What is he into?"

Brimly shrugged. "Don't know everything of course. But I'm pretty sure he runs narcotine, from a supplier out west past Calas."

"Truly." Raedrick's voice took on an icy undertone.

"That's what I've heard." Brimly gave first Raedrick and then

Julian a meaningful look. "There's no proof of that, mind you. Just rumors." He took another sip from his glass. "But he always surrounds himself with sketchy people."

"He doesn't sell here," Julian said, trading glances with Raedrick. "We would have seen signs."

Brimly nodded. "Not enough money here to make it worthwhile. Out east, though, in Mangin City or Pepperidge... Lots of potential customers there."

"So his legitimate trading is just a front."

Brimly crooked an eyebrow at Julian and shook his head vigorously. "No, I don't think so. The drug is... Icing on the cake, if you will."

Horace had been silent for a while, but the more Brimly said the deeper his scowl grew. "Why do we trade with a man like that?" His sounded as though he would like nothing better than to grab Sarillo and tear his ears off.

Julian couldn't say he blamed him. Above and beyond being a complete ass, if Sarillo really was involved in the narcotine trade... Julian had seen good men laid low by the drug, losing everything—their money, their sanity, maybe even their souls—to their addiction. Men who traded in that sort of misery had a special hell waiting for them.

A special hell.

Brimly gave Horace a look that screamed, "Stop being an idiot." But he said, "We don't get enough caravans coming through here anymore that we can pick and choose who we deal with, do we?"

Horace scowled all the deeper, but he nodded grudging agreement.

"I don't understand," Julian said. "Meaning no offense, but if *you* know about his dealings, how come - "

"How come the authorities don't put an end to him?" Brimly shook his head. "His family is connected. He crosses the right palms with gold. Or the authorities are just blind? I don't know."

He drained the last of his whiskey. "But that's not your concern. *Your* concern is finding that thief. Any progress?"

Raedrick and Julian traded looks. "Not really..." Julian began, but Raedrick ran over him. He quickly summed up Bart's discovery at the crime scene and Melanie's theory about the magical construct.

Brimly frowned thoughtfully and tapped his fingertips along the top of the table. "That's not a lot to go on."

Julian, grudgingly, nodded agreement.

Brimly blew out a deep sigh and looked to the side, out the window overlooking the lake. "We're never going to get that tax money back."

Raedrick perked up. "So you and Danil came to an agreement?"

Horace looked between the two of them, confusion mixed with something deeper—hope?—on his face.

Brimly nodded. "He wanted me to make good on all that was taken, but that would have drained most of the tax money I've been saving. As it was, he settled for four hundred marks. Said that would keep them through the first catch, maybe a little further."

Four hundred marks? That was... Well that was more than Julian expected to ever see in his life.

Horace's mouth dropped open. "What?"

Brimly looked at him, a mixture of amusement and consternation on his face. "Danil hasn't told you yet?"

Horace shook his head.

The Mayor rolled his eyes. "I'm fronting the company a loan out of all that tax money I've been collecting over the years, so you all don't fold between now and the first catch." Under his breath, he added, "And it'll probably land me in a dungeon somewhere."

It was like the light of Heaven had shone on Horace's face. A pallor of defeat had been resting on him, but it fled in the face of the Mayor's news. Suddenly he was grinning from ear to ear. "That is - "

The Mayor scowled at him and jabbed a finger in his direction, very nearly poking him in the nose. "So you tell those idiots who work with you to cool off. They'll get their damn money, and I don't need them beating on people who are here to help the rest of the town make their money as well. Hear me?"

Horace's smile faded and he nodded. "Aye, Master Mayor. I'll get my boys in line, but I think you've done the hard work on that front."

Brimly just harumphed softly.

Raedrick traded a long look with Julian. He knew exactly what his old squad leader was thinking. If it would take four hundred to keep them through, how much…

"How much did the thief actually take?" Raedrick asked, for them both.

"Eh? Oh." Brimly gave a little shrug. "Danil said it was almost a thousand marks. Don't know why he thought I'd be willing to part with that much, but - "

"Rae," Julian said, not noticing or caring that he had just interrupted the Mayor. "You know what that means?"

Raedrick nodded immediately. He saw it, alright. Julian felt his spirits lift for the first time in a while; their task had just become a lot easier.

The Mayor scowled at them, clearly liking not knowing what they hell they were talking about even less than being interrupted.

"There had to be more than one thief," Raedrick said.

"How's that?" said Horace.

"Do you know how much even a hundred marks weighs?"

The old Fishing Man blinked, then his eyes widened. So did the Mayor's.

Julian found he was grinning. "One person would have had a fairly easy time sneaking in and out of that place. But two? Or three?" He shook his head. "Somebody will have seen them, even at that hour of the morning. I expect when we go talking to the

Covington Brothers' neighbors and surrounding businesses, we'll find someone who saw one of them, and probably didn't even know it."

"And it will make it that much harder for them to hide the money, or make a getaway out of town if they try to flee," Raedrick added.

The Mayor looked doubtful, but he said, "Well, get to it then!"

Julian rose from his seat, but Raedrick paused. He looked at the Mayor seriously. "Regarding Sarillo. You'll - "

"Yes, yes." Brimly waved Raedrick's words away. "I'll set him straight in the morning. If Molli hasn't already. You'll get no more trouble from his lot, or I'll make him wish otherwise."

Raedrick nodded and rose as well.

Brimly saw them to the door and bid them a courteous good night, but as the door swung shut, closing them out of his house, Julian found himself frowning, doubts flowing back into him.

They turned and began trudging back toward the main part of town, and he glanced over at Raedrick. "You really think Sarillo will listen?"

Raedrick shrugged, but Julian noticed he was frowning as well.

"I don't think so either."

## 17

## PAYDAY

Julian swung the cell door open and scowled at the sleeping man within. Here it was, well past sun-up and into the morning, and he gets to sleep in? Not in this cell block.

"Get up, Worly," he said, and strode across the cell to nudge the fishing man with his boot. "Time to go."

Worly jerked when he felt Julian's boot and lifted his head. He had stringy hair the color of hay and eyes of nearly the same shade. Squinting up at him, though, Julian could see his eyes were bloodshot.

Probably had a bit of a hangover. Served him right.

"Come on," Julian said a moment later, when Worly still hadn't moved to get up. "It's pay day. Get up!"

That got his attention. The fishing man pushed himself erect and rubbed at his temples with his fingers. "What're you talking about, Constable?" he mumbled, sounding tired and grumpy. "Ain't no money left."

"There is now. Get up and get your behind down to the warehouse. You'll miss it if you don't hurry up." That was not strictly speaking true; Danil and a couple of his men planned to be there all day, or until everyone got what was coming to them. Or at least that was what he said. But Julian didn't need Worly loafing around his cell block all day; he had things to do.

The prospect of getting paid lit a fire under Worly, and while he didn't exactly leap to his feet, he got there in a hurry. He walked slowly to the cell door and turned left, toward the front office of the Constabularly. He scowled at Farley as he passed his cell. "You gave it back?" he said, incredulously.

"He never took it, you oaf," Julian said, and gave him a little rap on the back of the head. "Now get out of here, and stop being stupid."

He watched Worly depart and shook his head. How some people managed to get through life without harm from all the stupid things they did baffled him sometimes. And speaking of stupid…

"You too, Farley. Time to go." He pulled the caravaner's cell door open.

Unlike Worly, Farley had been up for a while. But he hadn't touched breakfast, or done or said anything. He just sat on his bunk with his head in his hands, looking thoroughly miserable. When the cell door opened, he raised his head, but made no move to get up or leave.

Julian rolled his eyes. "What? Need a written invitation? Get out of here, and don't cause trouble in my town again."

Farley still didn't move.

"If he don't want to go, I will," offered Geoff, from across the hall.

"Shut up, Geoff," Julian said over his shoulder absently. He kept his eyes on Farley. "What's the problem Farley?"

Finally, the caravaner spoke. "If it's all the same to you, Constable, I'll just stay here for a while."

"It's not the same to me. Get!"

"You don't understand. Cooper…" Just then, Julian realized Farley was trembling, and the paleness of his skin went beyond a natural northerner's skin tone. He was frightened. Very frightened.

Julian frowned. He had half a mind to kick the fellow out anyway, but if he really was as afraid as he looked… What the hell, he wasn't hurting anything sitting there for a while.

"Fine. Stay til you're ready. But if it's free meals you want, you can forget it. And you're not staying here tonight again either," he said, then he went back into the front office. He left the cell block door open.

Raedrick returned a few minutes later. When he came in, he took one look at the open cell block door then turned a questioning gaze toward Julian. He gestured toward the door, his expression asking the question for him.

Julian leaned back in his chair and shrugged. "Farley won't leave."

Both eyebrows climbed on Raedrick's head. "Truly?"

"Yup. He's afraid of Cooper." Julian leaned forward and frowned. "Deathly afraid. I haven't seen anyone scared like that since Jayme before that battle near Fiddler's Creek."

Raedrick returned the frown. "Well, we can't sit here all day." He tromped back into the cell block. His voice echoed back. "Farley, we have to go, and we can't leave the cell block door open with no one here. You either go now or you stay here until we get back."

Farley's murmured reply almost carried to Julian's ears. As it was, he could tell the man said something, but not what.

A moment later, Raedrick returned. He shared a resigned look with Julian, then shrugged and shut and locked the cell block door.

"Still won't go?"

"No. And that disturbs me a great deal."

Julian stood and put on his baldric, then settled his cloak about his shoulders. "Well we won't solve it staring at the walls here. Where to first?"

Raedrick looked back at the cell block for a few seconds, clearly mulling over Farley's situation. Then he shrugged. "I hear the line for payday stretches around the block at the Covington Brothers'."

That bore visiting, not just to make sure nothing *else* went wrong over there. Someone near there had to have seen something yesterday morning. It was time to find out what.

---

"Sorry, Constable. I've been racking my brain for the last day, trying to think of anything that might help, but I can't remember seeing or hearing anything that night."

The speaker was a plump woman named Nathalie who had maybe seen her twentieth summer. Nevertheless, she presided over a fairly successful seamstress shop that was based caddy-corner from the portion of the Covington Brothers' warehouse that housed its office space. She and her elderly mother, who had started the business before passing it on to her, lived atop the shop, and if anyone was positioned to see what had happened it was her.

Julian let out a disappointed sigh, but he managed to smile encouragingly at her. "Nothing at all? They would have been making their getaway around the time you got up."

She shook her head, sending her pin-straight black hair fluttering around distractingly. "Mother always needs help in the morning. If there was something going on outside, I missed it." She saw the look of frustration on his face and frowned. "I'm so sorry. I want to help, but..." She trailed off.

"No need to be. How could you know what was happening?" He smiled again, trying to look grateful for her assistance—and he was, but he would have been more so if she had looked out her cussed window that morning. "Well, I'd best be off. Thank you, Nathalie."

She smiled in return and bobbed a shallow curtsy which he returned with a slight bow from the waist. That made her smile widen, and by the time he left, she was back to her normal bubbly self.

His smile slipped as soon as the door closed behind him, and he sighed again. That was the fourth person on this block who had neither seen nor heard anything the morning of the robbery. How was that possible?

But he knew the answer. It was possible because the robbers had picked the exact right time to act. At that hour, people are either beginning to stir or on the edge of it. They aren't their most alert, but if they hear noises outside they think it's their neighbors getting started on their days, so they don't think about it. But, especially here in the Vale, and at this time of year—it's still dark enough that it's hard to make out details at that hour as well.

A well-planned and executed job, this was.

It was galling.

He turned left and crossed the street to where Raedrick was coming out of a building that housed half a dozen flats that fishing men without families rented. His eyes met Julian's, and he shook his head in the negative before Julian had the chance to ask.

Damn.

"Well, that got us nowhere," he said as he came to a halt next to his friend. "You'd think two or three men hauling a bunch of sacks that made clinking noises as they moved would have caught *some-one's* attention around here."

Raedrick frowned deeply as he nodded agreement. "We're missing something."

Down at the end of the block, the line of fishing men getting their month's pay had dwindled. It now only stretched halfway down the side of the building.

Julian started walking in that direction. "Well, let's go over it again. The thieves were there when Jakob came in early to get ready for payday."

Raedrick nodded. "That doesn't seem odd to you? Why do it that late in the night? It just risks someone walking in on them."

Good point. And a good counterpoint to his earlier thoughts about the timing of the crime. "Which is what happened." Julian chewed on that one for a few steps. "Maybe there was more money than they expected. They thought they'd be in and out, but there was so much they couldn't move it all at once, so they came back."

Raedrick shook his head. "Too much risk. You don't come *back* to the scene."

They were drawing near to the end of the block, and to the main entrance to the warehouse. There in the doorway, behind a desk he had set up for this occasion sat Danil, with Horace at his side. As each fishing man came up, Danil handed him a small sack and Horace pointed to a piece of paper lying atop the desk. The fishing man bent to sign his name or make his mark, then he went on about his business and the next fellow came forward.

Danil seemed remarkably composed for someone whose brother was lying in bad shape in the Healers Circle Guild House. But then Julian supposed he had to be; business couldn't stop because of one set of bad circumstances, and all those men still needed to be paid.

But still…

"Maybe taking the money wasn't the point."

Raedrick looked at him like he was daft.

"Hear me out." He came to a stop, watching Danil pay his men, and a little chill went up his spine. "Maybe Jakob was the target all along, and the robbery was just a smokescreen, to distract attention."

A frown was Raedrick's only response.

"Think about it. How many people know Jakob went in early on payday? Danil, surely. Who else? If someone had a grudge or wanted him out of the way for some reason, when better to lie in wait for him?"

Raedrick remained silent as he considered Julian's words, then he nodded slowly. "But why there, and why take the money?"

Now it was Julian's turn to look at him like *he* was daft.

"I know why someone would *want* to take the money,"

Raedrick said in an exasperated tone. "But why have that be part of the job? There are better ways to distract..." He trailed off and looked at Danil. His brows furrowed and he scowled darkly.

Julian nodded. "Exactly." He looked back at Danil as well, and all of a sudden it didn't seem at all odd that he looked so calm and composed. "It's a great scam. He gets rid of his brother, and has the perfect excuse why it wasn't him that did it. After all, he wasn't there. It *wasn't* him that did it; it was the men he hired who did the deed. And then we suckers tell the Mayor to give him even more money to make up for what was," he made quotation marks in the air on either side of his head, "stolen." He shook his head in admiration of the brazen nature of the plan, if for nothing else. "What odds do you give that money's sitting in his house right now?"

The scowl faded from Raedrick's face, and he shook his head. "There's just one problem."

"Besides it being diabolically brilliant?"

Raedrick made something that was half snort, half chuckle. "Why, oh criminal mastermind," he turned eyes toward Julian that were now mischievously teasing, "would the men who broke in not keep the money for themselves?"

Julian felt some of the wind go out of his sails. "Oh. Well, maybe they split it with him."

Now it was a full snort. "Do you think Danil could intimidate a couple of hired thugs into honoring an equitable split?"

He was forced to concede that no, that was unlikely. Reluctantly, he shook his head.

"So the point is moot. Whether it was supposed to be a robbery or no, a robbery is what it is." He cuffed Julian lightly on the shoulder. "I told you before Danil was a bad suspect."

Julian rubbed his shoulder, feigning injury and affecting a put-upon expression.

Raedrick just chuckled. After a moment, Julian followed right along.

The last of the fishing men picked up his pay and hurried

away. Julian noticed it was Worly. Their eyes met from across the street and Worly blanched, then spread his hands slightly and shrugged in a manner that could only be half-apologetic and half-embarrassed. He looked happy enough, despite it all.

That left Danil alone with Horace.

"Why don't we go talk to the bad suspect. See how things are going?"

Raedrick nodded, and they crossed the street.

# 18

## DELAYED COMMERCE

Horace and Danil were going over the paper that the fishing men signed as Raedrick and Julian approached.

"Did we miss anyone?" Danil asked.

"Nope, looks like..." Horace trailed off as he spotted them coming, and he gave them a welcoming grin. "Morning, Constables."

"Horace. Danil." Raedrick nodded in greeting. "Everything go alright?"

Danil looked up at them and nodded briskly. "Perfectly." From up close, he didn't look nearly as put-together as he had from afar. He had dark shadows below his bloodshot eyes, and he was unshaven. For that matter, it looked like he was wearing the same clothes as yesterday.

He took the papers from Horace and stacked them neatly. Then he picked them up and stood. "That should carry us through. And provided Master Sarillo has everything, and that he doesn't suddenly raise the price on me, we may just get through this mess." He sounded like he was trying to be upbeat, but his demeanor told a different story.

"When do you close the deal with him?" Julian asked.

"In about a half hour, then his people should deliver the goods after lunch."

Horace spat to the side. "Sooner we get done with that fellow, the better."

Julian was inclined to agree. On the other hand, if some of his hands were the culprits, they could not allow that caravan to leave town. Not yet.

Leave it to Raedrick to come up with a solution to that problem. "Is there some way you can delay the transaction?"

Horace shot him an incredulous look, Danil an affronted one.

"I don't know," Danil said. "I suppose. But why would I want to?"

"Once his business is done, he's going to want to leave," Julian said, giving his partner an approving grin. "We need them to stay in town, at least until we're sure none of his men were your robbers."

Comprehension shown through Danil's eyes, but he frowned uncertainly. "I'm not sure what excuse I can give. It's not like I can claim poverty anymore, not after this morning."

There was that. Julian scratched at his chin, but he had nothing to offer there.

Apparently neither did Raedrick. "See if you can come up with something," he said, in his gentle-order voice, the one that said maybe you don't have to do this, but if you don't you might really make me unhappy, and you wouldn't like it if you made me unhappy. Julian had heard that sort of tone many times, but mostly from women before he met Raedrick.

He made a note to tease him about that later.

In the meantime, though… "How's Jakob doing?"

Danil seemed to welcome the change in subject. But only for a second. "Master Sebastini says he's doing better, but he looks the same to me. He just lies there…" His shoulders slumped, and his bottom lip began to tremble.

Oh boy. He hadn't meant to bring Danil to tears.

Horace gave Danil's shoulder a gentle squeeze, and that

seemed to buck him up. He drew a deep breath and gathered himself, then he wiped the tears from his eyes and gave Horace a nod and a look of gratitude. Then, unexpectedly, a crafty smile appeared on his face.

"If you'll excuse me, gentlemen," he said, "I think someone said his condition has changed. I'd better go check in with Master Sebastini." He sniffed softly. "Horace, can you close up for me please?"

The old fishing man nodded, a matching grin growing on his face. "Happy to."

Danil passed a key ring over to him, then, papers still in hand, he gave Julian and Raedrick a quick nod and maneuvered around the desk, then to the street. He set a brisk pace toward the Healers Circle, and did not look back.

"Gotta hand it to him, ain't no way Sarillo can object to that reason for delay." Horace chuckled softly.

"No, he certainly can't," Raedrick agreed. "Need some help with that desk?"

Horace nodded. "Sure."

It only took a couple minutes to get the desk back inside and situated in rear of the warehouse's main room. Then Julian paused to take a look around.

It was clear Danil was trying to move on, get things squared away and ready for the delivery. The shades were drawn, and sunlight streamed in through the windows, illuminating the work floor. A wide space in the center, before a pair of carriage doors, had been cleared out in preparation.

Two muscular men in one-piece working attire, who Julian recognized as the warehouse foremen, were just finishing moving a tool bench to the side when they brought the desk back. The foremen knuckled their brows to Raedrick and him, and nodded to Horace in greeting.

"Delivery may be delayed a bit, boys," Horace said to them, and went on to explain the situation. They exchanged doubtful looks between each other, but shrugged.

"I guess send word when Danil needs us then," the taller of them, a dark-haired man named Borz said.

With that, the pair turned to leave.

"Hold on a second," Julian said, a sudden thought coming to him.

They turned inquiring eyes on him.

"Anything in the warehouse out of place?" They looked at him like he was daft—seemed like he was getting that a lot lately—and he added, "Besides the safe, I mean. Anything wrong on the floor when you came in?"

Borz pursed his lips in thought, and glanced at his companion, a dark-complected fellow named Kelvin. Kelvin shook his head and shrugged.

"Not that we noticed," Borz said.

"Ok. Thanks, gents."

They both nodded, then they walked briskly out of the warehouse.

Raedrick was looking at Julian oddly. "What was that about?"

"Well, it just hit me. Maybe the reason no one noticed two or three guys lugging big bags of coins around yesterday is because they didn't. Maybe when they found out how much was in that safe, they only took part of it, and stashed the rest. Somewhere close by, but out of sight. That way they could make a few more trips for the rest, but they wouldn't have to risk coming back to the actual scene. The easiest place would be somewhere here in the warehouse."

"And we didn't look anywhere except the office, because that's where the robbery went down," Raedrick said.

"Exactly."

Horace looked around the wide-open space, then shook his head. "Not many places to hide in here, Julian."

"True," Raedrick said, "but we should check to be sure." He nodded approvingly at Julian. "Good thinking."

"Thanks, boss," he replied, applying suitable sarcasm. That

earned him a long-suffering look from Raedrick that quickly faded beneath an amused grin.

Ten minutes later, he was not feeling quite so clever.

Horace was right, there were not many places to hide in the warehouse. It was designed for throughput, with the workstations arranged so the incoming fish could be brought in in bulk and processed as quickly as possible. So there really were not many nooks or crannies, and they were quickly able to search all of them.

And naturally they came up empty.

"Well, so much for that idea," Julian said.

"Not so fast, boy," Horace said. He scratched at his beard for a second. "If I were those thieves, I wouldn't want to leave it in here anyway. Unless I already worked here I couldn't just come back in, easy as I please." He gave them a level look, then added, "And none of our boys would do something like that."

"True." Raedrick frowned thoughtfully and looked around as though he could see through the walls to the street beyond. "Maybe someplace outside, but close."

Horace nodded. "Maybe." He looked out a window on the sunny side of the building and squinted up at the sun. "Hmm. Almost time for Danil's meet with Sarillo. Think I'll break the bad news to him."

"Tell him we said hi," Julian said, and Horace snorted in response.

The three of them exited the warehouse together, and Horace drew the door shut behind them. He fiddled with the keys that Danil gave him for a moment, trying first one than another until finally, on his fourth attempt, he found one that fit the lock.

He shook his head and chuckled to himself as he locked the door, and when he turned around, he said, "Damn key always gives me trouble. Looks the same as all the others, or I'm just getting old."

Julian snorted and gave him a light clap on the shoulder. "Come now, Horace. Compared to you, *dirt* is young."

The old fishing man scowled at him for a second, then laughed again. "I can still dance rings around you, boy." He tucked the key ring into his pocket and drew his cloak about himself. It was a bit more chilly than it had been yesterday, though still balmy compared to a week ago. But then, old people felt the elements worse than others.

"Well, I'm off," Horace says. "Luck, Constables."

Raedrick watched him stroll off in the direction of The Oarlock and shook his head. "I'm not sure what this town will do when Horace is no longer around to take care of it."

"Drown in ale that has no place to go, is what. You've seen him drink."

Raedrick laughed. "True enough." He narrowed his eyes and looked down the street. "Come on, let's see if we can find that hiding place."

# 19

# PRINTS IN THE SNOW

They turned left from the warehouse entrance and walked slowly down the road, retracing their steps from earlier. Snowdrifts still covered much of the area on the sides of the road, except for the paths that people had dug to allow entrance to the various buildings. As they walked, it struck Julian that they were being a bit overly optimistic.

"You know, Rae, they could have just dug out a hole in these drifts, put the money in there, and then covered it up again. We could walk past it a hundred times and never see it."

Raedrick shook his head. "They would have to mark it, or else they would never find it again either."

That earned him a snort. "Don't know about you, but I would damn sure remember where I buried a thousand marks."

"If you were in a hurry, and at night?"

He pondered that for a minute as they paused to let a group of children under the watchful eye of their teacher, Helena Winslow, pass ahead of them. Helena looked haggard, but that had been the case ever since her sister was killed last summer. Julian would have thought that time would heal the wound, or at least carrying on with their work would, but if anything she actually looked worse now than she had then. She was thinner, and always seemed to have dark circles under her eyes. Still, she managed a bright smile and a courteous nod as she led the children past, and from what he had heard the classes she taught were still top-notch, the children—and their parents—happy.

So maybe things were better than they appeared. She was doing the work of two now, and that caused a strain on a person's reserves. But if everyone involved was happy, herself included, was that really a problem?

He watched the teacher and her charges pass, and wasn't sure whether to pity or admire her. Or both.

"She carries a heavy burden," Raedrick said, and Julian could only nod in agreement. "It was one thing when Beverlee was alive; they had each other for support. Without her, and with no husband..." He left the rest unsaid.

"You'd think the other ladies would help her out," he said as they began walking again.

"Lani tells me they've tried, but she will have none of it."

"Stubborn."

Raedrick chuckled softly. "Takes one to know one, I suppose."

Julian just snorted.

They came to the corner where Nathalee's seamstress shop stood and stopped. To the left lay the back side of the warehouse, where the office was located. Directly across the street were two more businesses besides Nathalee's and another group of flats.

Julian had been to all of them earlier.

To the right, the branching street led down a shallow grade toward the docks, and the lake beyond. The flats Raedrick had investigated lay in that direction, and opposite them a butcher shop and a small place that was owned by a retired fishing man who now made mead. Pretty good mead, too, though to Julian's taste that meant it was just palatable. Still, for those who liked mead, it was choice stuff. After those few buildings lay Lake Road and the docks themselves. There was nothing obvious that looked like it could make for a hiding spot.

"I dunno, Rae. It was just a thought. I really don't see anything that could work. Maybe they're just big strong guys, or maybe the Covington Brothers had some of their money in jewels or something."

"I doubt it. They would probably have most of it in small coin, otherwise how would they pay anyone? Can't expect a man who makes a few silver a month to have change for a full mark lying around, can you?"

Which was a very good point. It just made the problem harder, though. "That means there would be even more bags to lug, so there either would have to be more of them or they'd make more trips. So how did people miss seeing them?"

Raedrick began to shake his head, but then his eyes alighted on the docks and he frowned thoughtfully. "Maybe they didn't."

Julian rolled his eyes. "Rae, have you been listening to people? No one saw anything out of the ordinary at all."

"Exactly."

He set off toward the docks and a vigorous pace, and Julian had to rush to catch up. "Where are you going?"

"How many people in this town would think it odd to see men carrying bags or boxes between the Covington Brothers' warehouse and the docks, even at that hour?"

It hit Julian like a thousand marks in pennies landing on his head. Hot damn, Rae was right! He grinned triumphantly and picked up the pace.

They reached Lake Road and stopped as they stepped out of the lee of the buildings and the wind picked up. All of a sudden, Julian considered that Horace was right about the conditions, and he hugged his cloak tightly about himself. That extra bit of breeze made a difference.

To the right, as the lake shore continued to the west, the town's finger piers stretched out into the lake like grasping fingers. Spaced about a twenty paces apart from each other and extending a couple hundred feet into the lake, even now they were crowded with crates, which no doubt held some of the equipment the fishing men would need when it came time to put the boats back into the water. The boats themselves, over twenty of them, were hauled out and resting on blocks along the shore to the left, their masts and rigging dismantled and their decks covered in tarps to keep as much of the elements off them as possible.

Julian had seen Horace's men out here all winter long, clearing what snow and ice had accumulated off of the boats after each snowfall, and had not envied them that task. But now, looking around with a different eye, he saw literally a hundred places the thieves could have stashed their plunder, if indeed that was what they had done.

That reduced his sense of triumph somewhat.

"We could spend a week looking through here and not find anything, Rae."

Raedrick seemed to have come to the same conclusion he had. The determined look he had worn just a moment ago faded; now he wore the look of a man with a long and unpleasant task ahead, one that he knew he had to perform but that he really would rather not.

"Hopefully we won't have to," he said after a moment's contemplation. "The robbers would not have had much time. I should think they would pick the quickest and easiest place they could find."

"Yeah." Julian gave a shrug, then, with a sigh, he headed toward Dock One, which lay almost exactly at the foot of the street they had just walked down. "In that case, I'll check out the dock."

Raedrick opened his mouth to say something, but instead he just shrugged and headed over to the closest of the boats.

The last few days of relative warmth had left the dock free of ice, so Julian had little trouble climbing the stairs up to its main span. But very quickly, he got the sense his search would end up being fruitless. He passed a multitude of boxes and crates, but as he checked them, one and all were either nailed shut or tightly secured with padlocks. He pitied the men who had to open them up, because a few of them looked like they were well and truly fused together from rust.

But aside from the crates, there really was no place to stash anything. He looked behind and around each one, and between them when they were stacked close together, and found nothing except for the wood planks that made up the dock's structure. It took him a while to reach the end of the dock, but by that time he despaired of seeing anything different, or finding any clue.

So it came as no surprise when that's exactly what he found: nothing.

He hunched his shoulders and turned back, then hunched them even further as the breeze struck him full in the face.

If he had been looking up instead of watching only his feet because of the wind, he would have missed it. And in fact, he very nearly missed it anyway. But when he was nearing the head of the dock and the stairs leading back down to Lake Road, he saw it.

The snow, largely unbroken around the base of the dock, was disturbed in one place on the eastern side of the dock, as though someone had plowed through the bank there and then pushed the snow back into place afterwards.

He frowned and stepped to the rail that lined the edge of the dock and looked over. There, in the snow that still covered the frozen surface of the lake, were footprints, leading from that broken area and out onto the ice. Underneath the dock.

A shiver of adrenaline went up his spine, and he leapt down the stairs to Lake Road in a single bound. He waved over at Raedrick, who was just emerging from underneath the tarp on a nearby boat.

"Rae, get over here! I've found it!"

## 20

# HIDDEN IN PLAIN SIGHT

Raedrick looked over the railing and nodded appreciatively. "They did a good job repacking that drift. You can't really tell the difference between that spot and the rest from the road. But..." He looked around again, out to the expanse of the lake, where even now some of the shacks that a few enterprising souls had set up out there still stood, despite the turn in the weather. Julian had tried to join Horace and a few of his friends ice-fishing a time or two, and aside from the ale involved he didn't really see the appeal. But there were a number of fellows, and a few ladies, in town who swore by it.

"I know what you're thinking, Rae. But folks who go out to skate or fish leave from the ends of the docks, not from the shore there. And why would they conceal the path they took if that's what they were doing?"

"True enough." He leaned way out, following the newly-discovered tracks as they disappeared beneath the dock. "I don't think we want to take their path. We don't want to leave any sign we were here."

"Yeah. But there's enough tracks down there that ours won't make a difference. Is there some rope in those boats?"

Raedrick grinned widely.

Ten minutes later, they had a pair of ropes tied to the railing and dangling down to the surface of the ice below. Julian kicked his leg over the rail and took hold of his rope, then paused as he looked down.

"You know, if we fall and the ice gives way…"

Raedrick snorted. "We're ten feet from shore, and it's a drop of less than ten feet. Plus it's probably frozen straight through to the bottom."

"Famous last words."

But there was nothing else for it. And he was sure Raedrick was right. Well, mostly sure. So he slipped his other leg over and rested his feet on the planking of the dock, outside the rail. Then, with a quick inhalation, he took firm hold on the rope with both hands and slowly, hand over hand, lowered himself down.

The snow crunched beneath his feet as he settled onto the ice, which of course held. He never really doubted it would. Never.

Raedrick landed a moment later and brushed his hands off on his pants, and they got to searching.

It didn't take long to find what they were looking for. There, tucked beneath the planking of the stairs, on the frozen ground beneath, were a half-dozen round lumps of snow. Too round to be natural and besides there was significantly less snow beneath the dock than to its sides, and even less directly under the stairs.

"Somebody didn't want this found," Julian said, that feeling of triumph welling up again. He squatted down beneath the stairs and brushed the snow away from one of the round objects. To his right, Raedrick did the same with another one.

The snow removed, the objects were canvas sacks filled with hard round, hard objects and cinched closed with leather draw-strings. Julian untied the knot on his string and pulled the sack open.

And gasped.

"Well, that answers that," Raedrick said.

Julian could only nod mutely. He had fully expected to see the sack's contents. But at the same time, he had never seen so much money in one place, or really ever. Gold and silver, but mostly copper and iron pennies, the sack was full to almost overflowing.

He turned his head and grinned at Raedrick. He got his voice back and managed to say, hoarsely, "We've struck it rich."

Raedrick snorted—or was that a chuckle?—and flashed a quick smile. A second later, the smile faded and he pushed back from the sacks, standing upright. "Close it up and push the snow back over it."

"What are you - ? We need to return the money."

"Yes. But if we do it now, we'll never catch the robbers."

And that was the clincher. The robbers had left the money stashed here to retrieve at a more convenient time. They would, no doubt, be back for it. But if word got out that he and Raedrick found it and returned it to Danil, they wouldn't show their faces anywhere near the stash again. They would head off with however much they managed to get away with two nights ago, and never be discovered.

He sighed and nodded, the closed the sack up and brushed the snow back.

The two of them went back to their ropes and hauled themselves up. By the time he reached the top of the dock, Julian's arms were burning with exertion and he was slick with sweat. "Son of a… I always hated that," he groaned as he flipped over the rail and collapsed to the wooden floor of the dock.

Raedrick nodded agreement, and for a short while they sat there, recovering.

"We're going to have to watch this dock like a hawk. Can't take our eyes off it for a minute if we want to catch those guys when they come back."

Raedrick nodded again.

"They probably won't come back until nightfall. I sure wouldn't." He sighed. "It's going to be a long couple of nights, I guess." Or maybe not so long, come to think of it. "At least Leminster offered to help. That'll make it less - "

"I don't think that's a good idea."

Julian blinked, confused. "What? They're Marshalls. This is what they do, Rae."

His partner was silent for a long moment. When he spoke, it was in a deadly serious, quiet tone. "Right now, no one knows about this but us. If we tell anyone - "

"You can't think Leminster and his boys will tell everyone. Why would they?"

Raedrick looked at him, and his gaze gave Julian a chill. "The robbers were from out of town, Julian." He emphasized the out of town, and Julian felt that adrenalin surge again.

He shook his head in denial. "They're law men."

"And they will understand if we hold this one close to the chest. But we don't really know them very well, do we. And they've been traveling with Sarillo for weeks, crooked as we know him to be, and they either haven't noticed he's bad news or they've been ignoring it." He have a quick shake of his head. "No. Until we know for sure who the culprits are, no one can know about this but us."

Julian opened his mouth to speak, but Raedrick cut him off.

"No one."

He had to admit it made sense. In a trust no one, suspicious sort of way. He was actually surprised Raedrick went there. Between the two of them, he had always been the quicker to trust, even when it was downright stupid to do so.

Julian supposed even the stubbornest of old dogs could learn a new trick or two, after all.

He still wasn't sure he fully agreed, or that he was comfortable with it, but he nodded reluctant acquiescence. "Ok," he said. Then, with a groan, he pushed himself to his feet and started untying his rope from the rail. "Let's get these ropes stashed and get out of here before someone asks what we're doing."

❧ 21 ❧

## LUNCH DATE

Julian slid Geoff's lunch under the door of his cell and stepped back. "Come and get it," he said with a grin.

Geoff just glowered at him, as usual. Also as usual, he did not make a move toward the food. Julian just shrugged; in a couple hours, the tin would be empty and ready for him or Raedrick to pick up. Geoff just liked to put on a show of defiance, for some silly reason.

He looked over his shoulder into the other cell. "Are you ever going to leave, Farley?"

The caravan man sat there, much as he had been when they left before, and shook his head.

Julian rolled his eyes. "Suit yourself," he said, then he went back to the front office. Like before, he left the cell block door open.

"He still won't leave," he said as he flopped down into his chair. "What the hell did Cooper do, do you think?"

Raedrick frowned at the cell block door. "Don't know. Maybe nothing; he has a wicked look to him, and is probably very good at being intimidating. Sometimes that's enough to cow a man."

Julian slid his chair a bit closer to his desk and opened his own lunch tin. Boiled potatoes and spiced fish—not fried, thank the

117

gods—with a hunk of bread on the side. Yummy. He bit off a bit of the bread. "He sure wasn't backing down to Worly last night."

"Well, Worly isn't exactly the most imposing person ever. And he didn't have time to think on it; he just reacted."

And that was a fair enough point. And really, it was none of their business. And as long as Cooper didn't actually make good on any threats to harm anyone within the Vale, there was nothing they could do about it anyway, except ask politely for him to be nicer to people.

Like that would happen.

"When did Leminster say he was coming over?" he asked, between bites of fish. The spices were especially zesty today.

"As soon as they finish eating. He's got some news for us, or something."

They had split up after leaving the dock, Julian back to the Constabulary to check on the prisoners and try to get Farley to leave, Raedrick to The Oarlock to pick up lunch. When he came back with the tins and the word that the Marshall wanted to have a palaver, Julian thought maybe Raedrick had rethought his notion of concealing the stashed money.

Nope.

"Remember, not a word," he said quietly, lest the sound carry back to the prisoners' ears.

"Yeah, I got it. I think you're going a little far with this one, but I got it." Julian washed down some of the spices with a mouthful of ale.

The sound of boots on the stairs of the front porch carried through the door, and a moment later the latch turned.

"Must be Leminster now," Raedrick said, starting to rise from his chair.

The door burst open, and three men burst in. Cooper was in the lead, and behind him were two other men who had the look over caravan guards about them. Muscles. A beard and a goatee. Scars. Leather armor that had seen better days. Sheathed swords. All three of them wore dissatisfied scowls, Cooper most of all.

He stopped in the middle of the front office and rested his hands on his hips. His gaze moved from Julian to Raedrick quickly, but Julian had the impression they had both been thoroughly measured even in that brief look.

"Constable, where the hell is my man?"

Raedrick shrugged and gestured toward the open cell block door. "We've been trying to release him all day, but he refuses to leave."

Julian added, "For some reason, I get the impression he doesn't like you very much. Can't imagine why, you're such a charmer."

Cooper glared at him for a second, then jerked his head toward the man behind him and to his left, the fellow with the goatee. "Harl, get him out of there."

Harl gave a quick nod, then started toward the cell block.

"I trust, Cooper," Raedrick said evenly, "that his fear you'll hurt him is misplaced."

Cooper made a dismissive sniff. "Bit overdramatic, that one. Always has been. I don't back away from needed discipline, but I don't hurt no one who don't need it."

Which was vague enough, and not exactly reassuring.

From within the cell block, Harl's voice issued forth. It was surprisingly high-pitched, coming from a big lug like him. "Get out here, Farley. We've got a delivery to make."

Some whimpering response, a bit too quiet for Julian to make it out.

"Oh for the love of... Come on. Don't make me drag you out." Sounds of a scuffle. "Tomas!"

The bearded tough with Cooper rolled his eyes in consternation and glanced at his boss. Cooper jabbed a finger toward the cell block door, and Tomas tromped forward. A few seconds later, the two fighting men returned, dragging a limp Farley between them.

Farley's heels dragged on the floor and he squirmed in their grip, but aside from being reluctant, even afraid, he did not appear hurt. All the same, Julian rose to get a better look.

Cooper shook his head and approached Farley, and the caravan man flinched back. "Quit sniveling," Cooper growled at the man. "You've got work to do."

Something crossed Farley's face. Several somethings. Apprehension, followed by relief, followed by reluctant acceptance. He placed his feet more firmly on the ground and pushed himself upright, and the two toughs let go of his arms.

Cooper turned back to Raedrick and made a mocking little salute to him. "Pleasure doin' business with you, Constable." He made a similar salute to Julian, then he nodded to his men.

Tomas opened the door and Harl led the way out. Tomas followed, pushing Farley ahead of him. Cooper brought up the rear.

Julian followed along behind them, just to watch in case they decided to beat on Farley once they had left the Constabulary. But no, the quartet turned right and headed toward Main Street and, presumably, The Oarlock, where the caravan had its wagons parked. Probably they were getting ready to deliver Danil's goods.

The caravan men were approaching the paving stones of Main Street when two other men passed them by, exchanging nods with the group. Leminster and Bart, arrived at last. Julian felt safer already.

The two Marshalls mounted the stairs up to the porch and nodded greeting to Julian.

"Constable," Leminster said. He glanced back toward Main Street, where the four caravaners were just disappearing from sight around the corner. "No trouble, I hope?"

Julian shrugged. "Not too much." He led them inside and explained what had happened. "I'm not sure what to make of that Cooper. I mean, he's clearly an ass, but the way Farley reacted to him makes me wonder if he's not also cruel."

Leminster stepped inside, followed by Bart, who shut the door behind them. The lead Marshal frowned at Julian's unspoken question. "Thing you have to understand about Cooper is he's new. Just signed on with Sarillo's crew. New security man feels a need to leave a mark quick, show everyone who's boss. A couple days out of Mangin City, he had one of the wagon drivers flogged in camp."

"In fairness," Bart said, "the man had been caught stealing from one of the other drivers."

"True enough," Leminster replied. "Still, Cooper was…rough… about it." He winced. "It made an impression."

"Apparently," Julian said, and found he was of two minds about Leminster's story.

On the one hand, he was right: discipline needed to be enforced, and thieving couldn't be tolerated, especially in a trading company. But there were ways to do it that didn't involve beating men bloody. But then, a thief in camp was intolerable…

Damn it, he didn't like thinking that maybe Cooper wasn't so bad after all. It was much more fun to actively dislike him.

Raedrick was leaning back in his chair with a disapproving frown on his face. Leminster must have noticed it, because he nodded in Raedrick's direction. "I thought he went a little over-board, myself. But there was no long-term harm done to the man, and it was Cooper's business, after all. We weren't there to interfere."

If anything, Raedrick's frown deepened, and Julian couldn't say he blamed him. Law men were supposed to…uphold the law, protect the weak, that sort of thing. He couldn't imagine Raedrick or himself just sitting back for something like that if they consid-ered it excessive.

It takes all kinds, it seemed.

It looked as though Raedrick was not going to say anything yet, or if he was it would only put them in a bad way with Leminster, so Julian figured it was time to change the subject. "So, what did you want to talk to us about, Marshall? Did Job and Iven learn anything from their caravan friends about the robbery?"

Leminster blinked. "Eh? Oh." He shook his head. "No, near as they can tell, either the drivers and strong backs are very good liars or they have no idea who was behind your theft." He spread his hands apologetically, as though to say he tried his best. Then he looked away, toward the cell block. "I, uh..." He cleared his throat. "Actually, I came to make a little bit of a confession, and to ask for your help."

"Oh?" Julian looked over at Raedrick, who had leaned forward in his chair, his eyes narrowing.

"What kind of confession, Caperick?" Raedrick had only very rarely used Leminster's given name before; it was a sure sign of his displeasure that he had dropped the formal address now.

"I knew it, Rae," Julian said in a teasing tone, trying to lighten the mood a bit. "*They* took the money!"

No one went with the joke, and he let his teasing grin fade.

It was going to be one of *those* sorts of meetings.

## ❧ 22 ❧

## COVERT OPERATIONS

Leminster pulled one of the chairs away from the front wall and sat down between Julian and Raedrick's desks, facing the cell block. Bart did the same. It seemed an awkward way to have a conversation, so Julian pulled his chair around so he was sitting in front of the cell block door, that way they could all be more or less facing each other.

The Marshall took a moment to collect himself, then drew a breath. "We didn't, strictly speaking, come up here to retrieve your prisoner."

"How's that?" Julian looked, confused, from Leminster to Raedrick.

For his part, Raedrick looked only mildly surprised. "I wondered why it took four Marshalls to escort one man."

Leminster smiled thinly and nodded. "Normally doesn't. In point of fact, we're mostly here to keep tabs on the caravan. Sarillo…" He paused, as though considering his words. "Rumors have been circulating that he's not on the up and up, that he has some shady dealings."

"He deals in narcotine." Raedrick apparently had decided that if they were all going to be honest, why not just let all the dirty laundry air.

Leminster's eyebrows shot up, and Bart looked like he had been smacked across the face with a stick. "How - ?"

The Marshalls shared a look, and Leminster said, more calmly, "Where did you hear that?"

Julian shrugged. "The Mayor used to be in business, and has known Sarillo for a while. He had heard rumors as well." He shrugged. "We've never seen evidence of it while he's been here, though, I guess because we're such a small town. So there's not much we can do about it."

Leminster frowned deeply. Then he sighed. "I suppose I shouldn't be surprised you had heard something." He leaned forward. "But from what we've heard, narcotine is just a small part of his venture. Mind you, we have no actual proof, or we'd have taken him into custody already. So, I decided to kill two birds with one stone: check out Sarillo and retrieve your prisoner. Since he was coming up here, and then proceeding on the Calas, I could do both at once."

"But Geoff is set to be tried in Mangin City."

Leminster nodded. "He is. When we depart tomorrow, we'll turn east until we're out of sight of town. Then Bart will continue to Mangin City with your prisoner and Iven, Job, and I will double back. We'll follow Sarillo's caravan at a discreet distance, monitor its actions, and coordinate with another team of Marshalls from Calas to take him down."

Julian blinked. That was actually fairly clever.

"How are you going to monitor the caravan without being seen?" Raedrick asked.

"We have developed a source in the caravan who will pass information to us."

Bart interjected, "That's part of the reason Iven and Job have been spending so much time with the drivers."

Raedrick and Julian traded a long look. It sounded like they had everything under control. "So what do you need us to do?" Julian asked.

Leminster put on an ingratiating smile. "Here's where it gets tricky. Sarillo is on a tight timeline, and so are we. His contact in Calas will only be there until a certain date, and if they miss each other they will not be able to meet again for some months. We overheard him complaining to his bookkeeper, Jerit, that you are going to keep him in town past his drop dead date for departure. If that happens, this entire operation is ruined."

"You want us to let him go." Raedrick's voice was flat, decidedly unfriendly.

Leminster blanched a bit at the tone, but he looked directly into first Raedrick's eyes, then Julian's, and nodded. "He's making delivery to your fishing company this afternoon."

"He is?" Julian asked. He glanced at Raedrick, who frowned. "I thought that was delayed."

Leminster shrugged. "Apparently he's meeting with Danil Covington as we speak." Some delay; thanks, Danil. "He will make delivery immediately after they settle the deal. You need to let him leave on the morrow, without delay."

Raedrick shook his head emphatically. "I can't do that, Caperick. The thieves who robbed the Covington Brothers are almost certainly among his caravan. If we don't recover that money - "

"I am well aware of the consequences to your town if that business goes under, Constable," Leminster said, the ingratiating look gone now, replaced by one of impassable steel. "But the Mayor has already made the company good until they can bring in the first few catches, has he not?"

Julian nodded, reluctantly. A moment later, Raedrick followed suit.

"Then the immediate danger to your town is over. This operation," he swept out a hand in the direction where The Oarlock lay, "can help a dozen larger towns and cities whom he frequents get out from under the cloud of narcotine he leaves in his wake. And out from other, even less savory dealings." He narrowed his eyes. "Frankly, Constable, I think the wellbeing of those many thousands of the Crown's subjects outweighs Lydelton's relatively minor problems."

Raedrick's eyes narrowed angrily. "It may be minor to you, living elsewhere, but to the people of this town - "

"I'm not going to argue this with you, Raedrick. The simple fact is that this operation is of greater importance." He tried that ingratiating smile again. "Besides, if the robber *is* part of the caravan, when we take it down, we will recover the money as well. When that happens, we will see that the money is returned to its rightful owners, I assure you."

Minus a finder's fee, no doubt. But Julian was smart enough not to say that.

If Raedrick didn't stop grinding his teeth soon, he was going to be reduced to eating with a spoon for the rest of his life. He scowled darkly and looked away from Leminster, toward one of the windows looking out at the front porch.

Julian cleared his throat. "We already more or less threatened him if he tries to leave before we've finished the investigation. We don't have any other suspects and the investigation is nowhere near done. So if we go and change our minds all of a sudden, don't you think that will look suspicious?"

Leminster's grin became broader, more sly. "I've already thought of that." He looked at Bart and nodded.

Bart cleared his throat. "In a few hours, after the delivery to your fishing company, Sarillo's bookkeeper will approach you to make an offer. They will consent to a search of all of their conveyances and goods, in exchange for being allowed to leave first thing in the morning."

Julian blinked in surprise. "He will?"

Both Marshalls nodded, in unison.

"So Jerit is your mole," Raedrick said.

Now it was Leminster's turn to look surprised, but it only lasted a second. He inclined his head to Raedrick as though acknowledging his cleverness without saying it. Though in truth, it didn't take all that much deduction to figure that out.

Julian looked at Raedrick and saw he still did not approve of the plan. "It makes sense, Rae. If we know for certain they don't have the money, why keep them here?"

The look Raedrick gave him spoke volumes. They both knew why there would be no money in the caravan: the thieves had not yet retrieved it from its hiding place under the dock. But they could easily do so after the search was completed.

Julian gave a little shake of his head, hoping that Raedrick would take the next step in his head. It didn't matter if the thieves went back for the money after the search, because the two of them were going to keep a close eye on that money and nab whoever tried to move it. So what was the harm?

Finally, after what seemed like forever, Raedrick sighed, looked back at Leminster, and nodded. "Very well, Marshall. We will do as you ask."

The smile was back, this time looking far more genuine. "Thank you, gentlemen."

# THE LIMITS OF MAGIC

"Tell me you found a way to detect that fire construct."

Melanie looked up from her perch behind her counter and narrowed her eyes at them. The bell on her door hadn't even had a chance to ring before Raedrick had voiced the request, more a demand. And from the icy look on her face, she did not take kindly to either the abrupt nature of his words, or the tone in which he said them.

Julian followed closely on Raedrick's heels and flashed a smile Melanie's way, hoping to alleviate some of the rudeness he had shown. But if anything, that just made the scowl that had begun to form on her lips deepen.

Almost as soon as the Marshalls left their office, Raedrick had hurried out, not bothering to tell Julian where he was going, and practically sprinted to Melanie's Magical Crafts. He hadn't even bothered to close the cell block door. Between fixing that oversight and Raedrick's pace, Julian barely managed to catch up with him before he threw her door open and practically stormed inside.

If Julian didn't know better—and right then he wasn't sure he did—he would say Raedrick was desperate.

"Well? Did you find a way?"

Melanie shot daggers at him with her eyes and slowly closed

the book she had been reading. "I would appreciate it, *Constable*," the way she emphasized Constable said as much about how impressed she was with him—with them both—as her demeanor or tone ever could, "if you are going to break my door off its hinges, that you at least address me in a civil tone of voice. And politely."

Raedrick jerked as though physically struck. Then he glanced back at the door to her shop. In fairness, it wasn't broken, but it did hang ajar still. And the little bell atop it was dislodged from its perch, hence the reason it didn't ring. The realization of how he had been acting seemed to register, and Raedrick's face went red from embarrassment.

"Sorry Melanie," Julian said, stepping past his friend and trying a calming smile again. "He's had a rough afternoon."

"Truly. And that justifies you two behaving like a couple of drunk adolescents?"

The two of them? Julian hadn't done anything. What was she mad at him for?

"Don't do try your innocent act, Julian. It's unbecoming." She looked at the two of them the way Julian's mother always looked at him when he was little and he had done something wrong. Then she sighed, slipped off her stool, and stepped out from behind her counter. She strode over to the door and pulled it to, then, standing on her tip-toes, began re-positioning the bell.

"I'm sorry, Melanie," Raedrick said. "Allow me - "

The glare she shot him stopped his words in his mouth, and he clamped his mouth shut.

After a minute's tinkering, the bell was back in place and she stepped back, her hands on her hips as she appraised it critically. Then, still not saying anything else, she went back to her stool behind the counter, opened up her book, and re-commenced reading. She looked up at them quickly. "Shall we begin again?" That was more a command than a question.

And then she went back to reading.

Raedrick looked at Julian, still a bit flushed. But now he looked more amused than embarrassed. Julian returned the look and gave a little shrug. What was he looking at him for? He wasn't the one who had barged in like a buffoon.

Raedrick cleared his throat. "Ah… Hello, Melanie."

She looked up from her book and put on a smile of greeting that did not reach her eyes, which still flickered with annoyance. "My two favorite law men," she said, in a tone that did not quite drip acid. "How are things this afternoon? Find the robbers yet?"

She had to know they had not, or she would not have thrown that barb their way.

"We're…making progress."

"Oh? That's good to hear." She closed her book and set it aside, then clasped her hands together atop the counter, the image of customer service. Except for the glare. "What can I do for you?"

Raedrick rolled his eyes, now starting to look annoyed himself.

Before he could say anything more and step in it further, Julian stepped ahead of him. "We were wondering whether you'd managed to find anything about those constructs you told us about from Timon's notes. We're starting to run short on time and anything that could let us find the robbers faster would be of great help."

An eyebrow rose on her forehead. "Short on time? Is there some deadline I am not aware of?"

Julian told her about their meeting with the Marshalls, their suspicions about Sarillo and his caravan, and their impending departure.

"Ah," she said after he was finished. "That explains your abruptness, I suppose." Raedrick opened his mouth to speak but she pointed an index finger at him. "It does not excuse it." Julian was surprised she didn't wag it at them.

It looked like Raedrick was grinding his teeth again. "Melanie, please," he said, sounding pained.

She stared at him for a long couple of seconds, then spread her hands and rolled her eyes. "Fine." And just like that, the glare, the frostiness, the bitter disapproval was gone. No more need for them, apparently; she had made her point. "To your question, yes Timon had some notes about constructs and a means to detect them." She pursed her lips. "It's quite ingenious, actually. The spell will make any magical construct in a limited area glow with the incandescence of a small oil lamp."

Julian blinked. He had realized immediately what Raedrick was after as soon as he saw where he was going. But, truth be told, he hadn't actually thought she would have discovered anything, at least not this soon. And certainly not something that would work like that.

"It will? How?"

Melanie gave Julian a looked that said the explanation would be far too complex for one of his intellect to understand. "It's complicated. And apparently only rarely used, for obvious reasons."

Raedrick's annoyance was gone, replaced by a look of such eagerness he could be a little kid who had just been offered a chest full of candy. "But you can do it?"

Melanie frowned slightly, then, with a sigh, she shook her head.

It was like Raedrick's face was trying to slide off his head, it fell so quickly. "What? Why not?"

"I lack the required components to cast the spell."

"I'm sorry," Julian said, feeling as though he had missed something. Several somethings. "What?"

Melanie looked at him as though at a stupid child, and her lips pressed together with disapproval. Then she glanced at Raedrick, and threw her hands up in exasperation. "Seriously, you two." She looked up at the ceiling and mouthed some words, and Julian had the impression she was voicing a complaint to someone...anyone. When she looked down, she glowered at them both in turn. "I explained this to you both the first time we spoke."

"The first time we spoke, you tried to singe my face off."

Julian only *thought* she had been looking at him like he was an idiot before. "The second time," she said, through clenched teeth.

Raedrick held up a hand, no doubt intending it as a calming gesture. "Please explain." She turned her eyes on him, and he added quickly, "Again."

Melanie inhaled deeply, then blew out the breath very slowly, and Julian could see her forcing herself to calm. "Alright. I'll keep this brief, and use small words." She looked back at him. "Will that be alright?"

Right then, he saw the wisdom in not objecting, so he just nodded.

"Magic is more than just incanting some words and waving your hands around. The two of you could try that all day long and accomplish nothing."

"Well, yeah, but - " She glared at him, and Julian shut up.

"The words and the motions give the energy of the spell form and function, but the energy has to come from *somewhere*. It doesn't just appear from nowhere, that would be impossible." She drew a breath. "That is where the components come in. The spell takes the energy bound in the components and converts it into the form the incantation and motions direct. Didn't you wonder why I had to sprinkle you with silver powder to cast that concealment spell? Or don't you remember why I told you I couldn't just call lightning from the sky willy-nilly?"

"Because the components were too expensive," Raedrick said, recalling their earliest conversation.

Melanie nodded quickly. "The component must relate somehow to the desired outcome, and it is destroyed in the casting."

"But..." Julian was struggling with the concept. "Those things you used were all really small. We've seen you cast fire spells that were..." He left it unsaid; he didn't need to say it, they had all seen the effects of some of her more potent spells before.

She arched an eyebrow. "There is tremendous energy in material things. See that pendant over there?" She nodded to the far wall, where the pentagram pendants hung. "If all of the energy contained in the material making up that pendant were to be released at once, it would likely wipe the entirety of Glimmer Vale from the map."

That hit him like a ton of bricks. He looked at the little pendant, then back at her, and shook his head. "No." That was absurd. Impossible!

"Oh yes. Believe me when I say there is more power in the world than you ever thought to imagine, my friend."

Raedrick was frowning. "But if that's so, and the component is destroyed in the casting, why - ?"

"Why doesn't the Vale blow up with every spell?" She smiled faintly. "It is a controlled release, and most of the energy is not used. The component dissociates into its basic structures, and what is left is little more than diffuse dust. But even the small amount of material that is actually burnt to cast the spell is enough."

Raedrick nodded, but his frown remained. "But these constructs you describe, they don't use components. And I don't recall seeing Loran Haversted using any, last summer."

Melanie rolled her eyes. "Of course they do. It's just the components are *within* the construct. Each time it is used, some of the component is used up. After a certain number of uses, it becomes merely a trinket, no longer functional from a magical perspective. As for Vigilant Haversted," her lips twisted in distaste at the man's name, "the more highly placed members of the Magestirium learn a method to eschew components completely. When they cast, the energy for their spells comes directly from their own bodies."

Raedrick blinked. "Isn't that...dangerous?"

She nodded. "It can be. It requires a hearty diet, and keeping one's self in top condition. But even with that, if one were to over-extend..." She didn't say the rest.

Well, that was certainly more than Julian thought to learn this day. And interesting as it was, it didn't really help them with their problem did it?

"Well, we're back to plan A then, Rae." Hardly a surprise there. And really, why did they need to worry about a plan B?

Raedrick looked at him and nodded, frowning deeply. "I had hoped we could locate the construct when we search Sarillo's caravan. That way we could take the thieves into custody and not have to gamble. But," he sighed, "apparently not." He drew himself up and put on a business-like expression. "Thank you, Melanie. Sorry for being gruff before."

Her eyes twinkled in the lamplight and she smiled faintly. "My pleasure. I just wish I could be more help."

"You've done more than enough for us over the last year as it is."

She gave a little shrug.

Raedrick squared his shoulders and looked back at Julian. "I guess we'd better go back to the office so we can look surprised when Jerit comes in."

"Yup. But before we go, we should talk with Horace." He nodded at Melanie by way of farewell, and gave her his most dashing grin. Then he turned for the door, but not before he saw her roll her eyes, in mock irritation he was sure.

"Horace?" Raedrick said, moving to join him.

"Yeah. You think I want to search through all that stuff with only *you* for help?"

## ❧ 24 ❧

## TO SEARCH AND NOT FIND

The stable yard at The Oarlock was chock full. Between the caravan's four wagons, Sarillo's carriage, all the boxes and crates, and all of his men and their bags, it was hard to see how Molli's people could cram any more people or animals in. It made Julian wonder what would happen if more than one caravan were to arrive in Lydelton at a time.

Of course, things as they were that was not going to happen any time soon.

Sarillo stood in front of his caravan's goods, with Cooper, glowering, at his right side and Jerit on his left. He was dressed in blue and grey wool, with a light off-white cloak over his shoulders, in keeping with the day's warmth. It seemed each day since the caravan arrived had grown warmer than the last, and talk around town had begun to speculate on the prospects of an early Spring. They'd gotten one in the lowlands, why not up here in the Vale as well, for a change?

Sarillo looked none too happy as Julian and Raedrick approached. "We're ready, Constables, as agreed. Though I daresay my men will not be happy having their personal effects searched in addition to everything else."

"I don't really care if they like it," Raedrick said. "No one leaves this town until we are sure they are not responsible for the robbery."

Cooper, still dressed for a fight, though he had changed his shirt at least, simply stared daggers at them. For a moment Julian thought sure he was going to launch into another tirade about how his men didn't go for that. But, amazingly enough, he kept his mouth shut.

Raedrick peered around at the faces of the caravan men, and their belongings, and nodded. "We'll get started in a moment. I hope you don't mind, but we've contracted some help, to make things go faster.'

As though on cue, Horace turned into the stable yard, clad as usual in his grey cloak though today he wore a yellow wool blouse beneath it that almost made Julian's eyes bleed, it was so bright. What in heaven's name was that? He hadn't been wearing that when they had spoken two hours before.

Behind Horace came four other fishing men in their grey cloaks, but thankfully they wore less eye-wrenching attire beneath.

Sarillo eyed the approaching fishing men and scowled. "You cannot be serious."

Raedrick smiled pleasantly at him, then glanced up at the sun, which was on the tail end of its trek toward the mountains to the east. "We've got maybe an hour of sunlight left, Master Sarillo. More hands means faster work, and I imagine you want this done as quickly as we do."

Sarillo's scowl remained, but he nodded acquiescence. "Very well."

After a brief conference with Horace and his men, they got to work.

<hr>

Of course they didn't find the money. Horace and his men seemed disappointed, frustrated even, when the inevitable result came to pass. Julian tried to mirror their dejection to keep up appearances, and found it difficult to do. When he knew exactly where the thing he was looking for sat, pretending not to know grated at him.

All the same, when Horace's men gathered around at the end of the search, he put a frown on.

"Thank you, gentlemen," Raedrick said gravely to them. He looked for all the world like a man who had been frustrated at every turn, but who remained determined nonetheless. "We made good progress this afternoon." One of the fishing men shot him a look that screamed "Baloney", and he raised a calming hand. "We've eliminated many potential suspects. The more who we know did not do it, the easier it will be to find the culprit in the end."

They didn't look convinced. In truth, they all, Horace included, looked decidedly troubled. And, thinking about it, Julian understood.

If the caravan people didn't take the money, that meant someone else did. And the only other someones in the town were local people. Up until now, most in town were certain, whether they said so or not, that it was one of the outsiders who did the deed. Now, the prospect that a neighbor...maybe even a friend... had done this to them loomed large in their minds, and it did not sit well.

That was an angle Julian hadn't thought of. By playing along with Leminster's plan, they had cleared the caravaners, and opened the door to internal distrust and dissent.

How long until that began to show in trouble between the townsfolk?

Julian just hoped Raedrick was right, and the culprit really was in the caravan and would come for the money tonight. Otherwise, they might be in trouble come morning. Or at most in a few days.

Raedrick turned to Sarillo next. "Thank you for your cooperation, Master Sarillo. I hope you and your men won't harbor any ill will over this. We had to be sure." He smiled warmly. "You understand, of course."

Sarillo inclined his head, stiffly. "Of course."

Raedrick nodded. "First round for you and your men tonight is on us," he said, more loudly so that all of the caravan men could hear it.

From the expressions on the caravaners' faces, that seemed to go a long way toward mending whatever bridges had been in danger of being burned during their search.

The caravaners spent the rest of the light re-stowing their gear and re-packing the wagons for departure in the morning. Raedrick and Julian helped as best they could, but found themselves shooed away by the strong backs and drivers more often than not. After their third attempt to help was rebuffed, they traded looks.

"Man doesn't want help, man doesn't get help, I guess," Julian said with a shrug.

"I suppose so." Raedrick led him to the gateway leading from the stable yard out to the street, then, glancing around to make sure no one was in earshot, said. "I'll take the first shift at the dock tonight."

Julian looked over to where Sarillo and Jerit stood deep in conversation, near the foremost of the wagons. "I hope you're right about this, Rae. If it really turns out it's not one of them…"

Raedrick nodded. "I know." Away from the caravaners and without an audience to play to, the stress, and below it, doubt, in his voice was plain. "I don't want to think about what might happen if the thieves turn out to be some of our own." He shook himself as though to cast that thought aside. "Come relieve me at midnight. I'll be watching from the first of the boats."

Julian nodded, and they clasped hands. "Good luck, Rae."

"Thanks. You too."

He turned to go, and had almost disappeared around the corner before a thought struck Julian. "Rae!"

Raedrick turned around, a quizzical eyebrow rising on his forehead.

"You're not sticking me with the entire bar bill you just racked up for us. Hand over your share."

In spite of the seriousness of the situation, Raedrick laughed with gusto.

## STAKEOUT

Raedrick pulled his blanket around his shoulder and hunkered down, trying not to notice the steadily dropping temperature or the ice and snow that had accumulated in the bottom of the boat despite the tarp that had covered it for the winter.

At least the chill would help him stay awake, and hopefully alert.

He had only delayed coming to the dock to stop by his flat and grab a blanket, but even that small delay had filled him with nervousness. That was irrational, of course; it was still just twilight and the thieves would not be foolish enough to come retrieve their loot while there was still light out. But the unease remained until he finally reached the dock and saw that the snowbank remained unbroken.

It was only after he slipped in amongst the boats and slid beneath the tarp of the first one that the thought struck him that the thieves may have already come and gone, but repaired the snowbank as they had the first time. That sent a shiver of panic up his spine, and he had to force himself not to bolt from the boat, over the snowbank, and below the dock to verify the money was still there.

It was irrational, that impulse, but it still took a while to put it from his mind.

He adjusted himself on the planks of the boat's deck; it was impossible to find a comfortable perch and keep himself positioned to look out from beneath the tarp and keep from noticeably displacing the covering in the process.

Another thing that would help keep him awake.

Time passed slowly, each minute seeming to last an hour as twilight quickly faded, replaced by the dark of night and the countless stars in the night sky. The moon would not rise for several hours yet, and this time of year the Lamplighters Guild did not light the lamps on the docks themselves; no need for it. So it promised to be a dark shift.

All the more reason why this would be the time the thieves chose to return. Plus, they would want to get the loot from its hiding spot and packed away in their wagon or on their packhorses before it got too late, so they could get some rest before the caravan's departure in the morning.

He had taken the first shift for that reason. Julian was a good man; the best Raedrick had ever known. But he was not as good at being stealthy as Raedrick was. He would need to follow them back to The Oarlock, identify them, and then rouse Julian and the Marshalls to make the arrest, and he didn't want to risk alerting them in the process.

He firmly pushed from his mind the notion that the thieves may, in fact, not be of the caravan. It was too dreadful a notion to think about, at least for now.

They could cross that river when they came to it, and may the gods grant they never would.

***

The look on Molli's face when Julian tossed down enough coin to pay for the caravaners' first round was a mixture of incredulity and amusement. "You been drinking already, Julian?"

He snorted. "Rae's idea, not mine. To ease their egos after having to endure a search of their things."

Molli sniffed as though she disapproved. But she took the money. "Ok. First drinks for the lot, on you two." He smiled teasingly at him. "But I think I ought to have a talk with the Mayor. You boys are getting paid too much."

He rolled his eyes. "Could you have one of your people come knock on my door a half hour before midnight?"

One of her eyebrows rose and she gave him a searching look.

"Official business, Molli. Just leave it at that."

She nodded slowly, a look of understanding on her face. And he wouldn't put it past her to have figured the entire caper out just from that; she was quick. Had to be, to have run this place successfully for as many years as she had.

He grinned warmly at her. "Thanks, Molli."

She returned the grin and gave him a light smack on the thigh with the towel she was carrying. It hurt a little, but he kept the grin on his face as he made his way through her taproom and out the door.

Once outside, he let the grin slip, and he hurried from The Oarlock's grounds to the street beyond, the turned left. Five minutes later found him outside the building where his flat lay, on the second floor above Fedwyn's Canvas Shop. He mounted the stairs two at a time and wasted no time in going inside.

It was not yet past twilight, but he needed to get some sleep if he was going to be any use at all after he relieved Raedrick. He was not yet particularly sleepy, but that should not prove a problem. In the Army, he had learned through hard experience how to grab sleep whenever the opportunity arose.

Sleep was a weapon, and sometimes in the Army hard to come by, so a good soldier learned to get it whenever he could. It turned out, a good Constable sometimes needed that skill as well.

Once inside, he stoked the embers in his little wood stove and threw in a couple pieces of split wood that he kept in a pile near the door. Then he stripped down, flipped over a five-hour hour-glass he kept on his bedside table, and lied down in bed.

And was completely unable to get to sleep.

He tossed and turned, tried counting to a hundred in his head, tried thinking about the boring book he had tried to read the previous month. It had put him to sleep every time then, but now it didn't help at all.

Of all the times for nerves to cancel out his ability to sleep. He had slumbered like a baby the night before a dozen different battles, but now...

He ground his teeth, forced his eyes closed, and cleared his mind.

And a second later, found himself going over all the things that could go wrong with the plan. The thieves had gone back for the money during the day, despite what seemed smart to do. They had found out that he and Raedrick discovered the stash and decided to quit while they were ahead.

They turned out to be locals.

Try though he might, he could not get any of it from his mind, and sleep would not come. Finally, in exasperation, he sat up and looked out his window. To the west, a faint glow on the horizon portended moonrise. The five-hour glass was two-thirds empty.

There were still a couple hours until midnight. He should try again to get some sleep.

But that was going to be futile, and he knew it. Better to get some food into his belly and get moving. The energy from the food would help keep him awake, and he had endured long nights before. He would just have to do so again tonight.

So he put his clothes back on and picked up his baldric. After a moments' thought, he also donned his mail before pulling a dark-blue wool coat over his head and slinging the baldric across his chest. Finally, he threw his cloak over his shoulders. Then he pulled his door open.

Back to The Oarlock he went.

Raedrick stifled a yawn and shifted on his seat again. The hours had been dragging by, with little to show for them except for aches in his back and legs and a chill that seemed like it would never go away. The only activity near the docks had come an hour into his vigil, when two of Horace's fishing men, quite tipsy by the look of them, stumbled down Lake Road, arms over one another's shoulders and singing a terribly off-key ditty.

Since then, nothing.

He rubbed at his eyes and worked his jaw, shifted again, pulled the blanket closer about his body—each movement just something to do to keep himself from drifting off to sleep. He needed to keep alert, but not for much longer.

Poking his head up past the tarp a little bit more, he looked to the west. The pre-glow of moonrise was brighter now. The moon would be up soon, and about an hour after that Julian would relieve him.

Just about an hour more, then he could rest.

That should not have been so appealing. The urgency of the night's mission and his desire to bring the thieves to justice should have been enough. Maybe if he were one of the gods, it would have been. But the hour was late, and he was having trouble keeping his zeal as weariness closed in around him.

From somewhere up the street, a door slammed and a pair of shouting voices carried to his ears. A lovers' quarrel, from the sound of it, though he couldn't make out any specifics. Not that it was his business anyway, as long as it didn't come to blows.

Fortunately, that sort of thing was rare in Lydelton. Although, hearing the sounds of the fight, he recalled the time late last summer when Bili Fredemyn's wife beat him with a frying pan so badly that he ended up spending a week in the Healers Circle under Ravi's care.

They had two small children who lived in fear of her outbursts. Bili had been able to keep them under control for a while, but they had grown worse until finally, the frying pan incident brought it all to a head.

That had been a dilemma, though. How do deal with it? They couldn't leave the children in that situation, but what to do with them? And how to make sure Freda never did that sort of thing again?

Eventually, Bili's parents had taken him and the children in, and Julian and Raedrick had ordered Freda to keep away from the children except under supervision. Of course, she had refused to hear of it, and it had taken a lecture from the Mayor himself and threats to throw her in prison for attempted murder—because that's what she had done to Bili—before she acquiesced.

But even now, they sometimes had to deal with trouble of some sort or another from her. It was…

A new noise jerked Raedrick out of his reverie. The crunch of boots punching through snow.

Someone was approaching, and not from the street.

He peered about, but could not see anyone. But then, his field of view was limited because of the tarp.

The sound of someone stumbling, and then the boat Raedrick sat within lurched suddenly. A man's voice cursed, from just behind him and to the right.

A second voice, pitched low, followed. "Keep quiet!"

They had come in through the collection of boats!

Raedrick pressed himself downward and slowly pulled the tarp more fully in place, silently willing the men to not see him there, to continue past in ignorance.

Through the small opening in the tarp, he saw the shadows shift, the shape of a head passing by. For a second, the head turned and Raedrick's breath caught in his throat. It was too dark to make out his features, but he had the distinct impression he was looking straight into the man's eyes.

His heartbeat pounded in his ears. Surely the man heard it?

Then the head vanished from his view as the man moved on.

More footsteps through the snow; Raedrick counted three men total. They were proceeding past him, toward the dock.

Slowly, ever so slowly, he pushed himself upward and moved the tarp aside so he could better see.

There, in the gloom, the trio had reached the stairs leading up to Dock One. They paused to confer for a moment, then the biggest of the three began tearing at the snowdrift, right where it had been displaced before. It only took a couple minutes to re-open the passage out onto the ice, and then the trio went down below.

Raedrick smiled thinly.

He had them.

❧ 26 ❧

# SPRINGING THE TRAP

When Julian returned to The Oarlock, he found the taproom mostly empty, a far cry from the bustle it had the previous two nights. The locals had all gone off to bed and, for a change, most of the caravaners had as well. That made sense; they were set to leave first thing in the morning. The lack of crowd was actually refreshing, after the last couple of days.

That was good, little chance he would bump into anyone who needed him, or the Marshalls. He could just have a quiet bite to eat and then…

But no, there they were, Leminster and Bart, at a table off to the right near one of the taproom's great fireplaces. Naturally, Bart saw him as soon as he stepped into the taproom, and nudged Leminster, who turned around in his chair to look his direction. Then he grinned and waved him over.

So much for a quiet meal by himself. But it wouldn't do to be rude to the Marshalls, so, with a sigh, he veered toward their table.

"Gents," he said as he drew near. "I figured you'd be abed already, what with your leaving in the morning and all."

Leminster shrugged. "A couple last ales for the road. Join us?"

"Don't mind if I do," he said, and sat down at an empty chair at their table. Movement to his left drew his eye, and he saw Tami making a beeline for them. He made a gesture like he was tipping a cup toward his mouth and she stopped, grinned, then turned toward the bar. "What time should we expect you to collect Geoff tomorrow?"

"We'll leave at a gentlemanly hour, say six bells?" Leminster hiccuped, and Julian wondered if he would even be awake by that hour. But that was the Marshall's business, not his.

"Sounds good."

Tami arrived a moment later with a tankard of tale, which she placed in front of him with a wide grin. He returned the smile. "Anything left of dinner, Tami?"

She pursed her lips in thought, then shrugged. "I might be able to scrape something up. But only because it's you."

Julian grinned more broadly and threw a wink her way. She gave a little giggle and patted his shoulder softly before turning away from the table.

He watched her walking away, and pondered that maybe Raedrick was right; she wasn't all *that* young, after all. He took a draw from his tankard and, upon lowering it, found Bart looking at him with bemusement.

"What?"

Bart shook his head. "I thought *Job* was a flirt."

Julian snorted. Job *was* a flirt, and the ladies were entirely too eager to fall for his lines than was probably good for them, or him. He wasn't sure why Bart would make the comparison.

Whatever. He decided to change the subject.

"I can't say I envy you, having to spend three weeks alone with Geoff."

Bart shrugged. "Part of the job." As if that would make it something other than a total pain in the behind for him.

"Yes, well, you'll deserve a bonus by the end of it." He took another drink, and something occurred to him. He looked over at

Leminster curiously. "Something I didn't think of before, when you told us your plan."

Leminster harumphed softly. "What's that?"

"Well, you said you were going to coordinate with another team out of Calas. That's a long ways off. Do you have pigeons with you or something?"

Leminster shook his head. "No, Iven'll take care of that part."

Julian blinked. That didn't make any sense. Across the table, Bart flinched, and he looked at Leminster reproachfully.

The senior Marshall seemed to regret what he had just said. He flushed and cleared his throat, looking away from Julian for a second. Then he met Bart's eyes—rather accusing eyes, those. The two of them seemed to communicate without speaking for several seconds, until Bart sighed and, shrugging, gestured toward Julian.

Leminster shook his head and muttered something inaudible under his breath, then met Julian's eyes again. "Well since I let it slip already…" He scowled, at himself more than anything else it seemed. "This cannot leave this table, hear me?"

That was intriguing. Julian glanced around; no one else was anywhere near their table and could possibly hear it. He nodded.

Leminster leaned forward, fixing Julian with an intense stare. "It's a special program we've got working with the Magestirium. They take some of our people and run them through a crash course, teach them some tricks to pass messages over long distances." His eyebrows rose. "We call 'em Communications Specialists, and it's done wonders for our coordination. Why, on this one case…"

Julian stopped listening. His throat had suddenly gone dry and his stomach clenched in a knot. "Iven studied at the Magestirium?"

Leminster stopped in mid-sentence and, giving Julian a strange look, nodded. "Yeah, for about four months. It's the standard - Hey!"

Julian was on his feet. This was bad. This was very bad. He had to tell Raedrick before it was too late.

He turned and sprinted for the door, passing Tami—again—with a plate of food on her tray and a startled expression on her face.

"Where are you going?" Leminster said from behind him.

He gave no answer, just shoved his way through the door and out into the night.

Raedrick kept close to the wall so as to remain in the shadows and crept slowly after the thieves.

He had waited as they returned, one by one, from beneath the dock, each hefting a pair of sacks, then watched as they crept past his boat and disappeared beyond his field of view. His gut told him to get out and get after them at once, but he forced himself to wait for a count of twenty, then slipped as quietly as he could out from under the tarp and off the boat.

At first, he saw no sign of them, and panic welled within him briefly. But then, in the faint light of the rising moon, he saw their footprints in the snow and, ahead, the profile of the last of them against a streetlamp as he slipped between two buildings and entered the street on the other side of the boats.

From there, a quick sprint brought him to that road, and he was able to keep them in sight the rest of the way.

They went un-erringly toward The Oarlock. Each step brought an increasing feeling of relief—relief that they were not townsfolk, after all—and triumph over the success of his plan. Now, watching from the shadows across the street and half a block down from the gateway leading into The Oarlock's premises, he could not suppress a grim smile.

The trio gathered against the wall surrounding the inn and conferred, then one of them put down his sacks and slipped inside. A moment later he returned and hefted his sacks again. Then he re-entered. After a half minute, the second man slipped inside.

It was time for Raedrick to move. The Oarlock kept lamps lit within their courtyard and premises, but the rest of the street had only sporadic lighting, and he had picked a place where the shadows were darkest to wait. Now, after the second man moved inside the gate, he sprinted across the street.

He stopped with his back pressed against the wall and watched the final man carefully. It was too dark, and he was too far away, to see his features clearly, but he obviously had not looked back in Raedrick's direction at all. His entire attention was on the interior of The Oarlock's courtyard.

Good.

Raedrick slid forward along the wall, closing his quarry. Once the thief went within, he would follow and see where he went. To the stables, most likely. He would note carefully which stalls and which horses the thieves used, then he would get Julian and the Marshalls and they would retrieve the money.

And then, on the morrow, when the thieves returned to make their getaway, they would make the arrest.

The man ducked inside the courtyard, and Raedrick hurried to the gate.

Peering around, the thief was more visible due to the lamps within. He wore a cloak with the cowl raised, and his back was to him, so Raedrick couldn't see who it was. But it didn't matter; he could not escape now.

He was making his way toward the stable, and Raedrick could see the light of lit lanterns from within its closed doors.

Perfect.

He slid within the courtyard and began following in the thief's footsteps, tasting victory on his tongue.

The front door to the Inn, the one leading into the taproom, flew open, shining light from the well-lit room within out into the courtyard. A man came dashing out at a full sprint, but he slid to a halt when he saw Raedrick.

It was Julian. What the hell was he doing?

"Rae!" Julian said, practically yelled. "Rae, we've got a big problem."

Ahead, the thief froze, then turned back.

It was Farley. He saw Raedrick and Julian and recognition immediately appeared on his face, followed by dread. His lips moved, mouthing a vile curse.

Then he turned and sprinted toward the stables.

Raedrick cursed as well and ripped his sword from its scabbard. "Damn it!" he snarled, casting a baleful look Julian's way. "Come on!"

To his credit, Julian had the grace to look abashed, mortified even, before Raedrick turned his attention back to the fleeing Farley.

The caravaner covered the distance faster than Raedrick would have thought he could have, encumbered as he was. He threw the stable doors open and darted within, shouting, "It's the Constable!"

Raedrick reached the stable a moment later and rushed inside.

And nearly had his head taken from his shoulders.

He heard the blade whistling through the air more than saw it and rolled to the side, coming back up on his feet and spinning to meet his attacker, sword at the ready.

And froze in shock when he saw who it was.

Job scowled back at him. "You should have left well enough alone." Then he advanced, his blade spinning through the air in a dizzying series of spiraling cuts that came so fast Raedrick could not keep track of them all.

## ❧ 27 ❦

# GETAWAY

**R**aedrick retreated from Job's attack. It was too fast, there was no way he could parry it.

The Marshall's sword whistled in front of him, just missing his nose, and he leapt backward.

His back struck wood; the door to one of the stalls. He spun to the left.

He heard steel striking wood and knew he had just barely escaped a second attack.

"Get a horse, Farley," a voice shouted, and he recognized it at once. Iven.

In all his imaginings, he never dreamed it could have been them. Oh, he had ordered Julian not to tell Leminster about the stash, but that was just to keep the secret as closely held as possible. To think that law men like these two would flagrantly betray their oaths like this...

No time to muse on that.

He backed away from Job again, this time managing a parry and a weak counter that kept the erstwhile Marshall from closing to closely.

Behind Job, Julian rushed into the stable, his longsword in hand and gleaming in the lantern light as though it were ablaze.

He looked about quickly, then advanced to someone on Raedrick's left.

Iven stepped forward into view from that side even as Job came on again.

Raedrick ducked beneath a cut and thrust forward, forcing Job to retreat. Raedrick was about to advance when Iven spoke rapid words in a language he didn't understand and thrust his hands forward at the advancing Julian.

Something struck Julian. Hard. He flew backward through the air and crashed into another stall, then slumped to the ground, either stunned or dead.

"Job!" Iven shouted. "Job, come on!"

Farley shot past, astride a horse whose saddle looked as though it had been fastened rapidly and poorly. It bounced around with each hoofstep, but the caravaner held fast, leaning against the horse's neck and kicking it to greater speed. Two sacks were tied to the rear of the saddle.

Job glanced at Iven and nodded, then came on again, his speed redoubled. Raedrick reacted purely on instinct and managed to parry the cut, but then Job was spinning around completely and Raedrick saw his leg rise.

Something struck the side of his head and Raedrick fell to the floor, dazed. His vision swam for a second and he saw stars, but he managed to roll onto his back.

Job stood over him, his sword tip pointed at Raedrick's throat, his eyes gleaming.

Raedrick swallowed and said a quick prayer to the gods; this was it.

Then Iven was there, astride a horse and holding the reins of a second in his hands. "Let's go!"

Iven tossed the reins to Job, and he caught them in his off-hand. "Don't follow," he said to Raedrick. Then he leapt up into the saddle and spurred his horse out of the stable.

Don't follow. Like hell.

Raedrick forced himself to his feet and took a step toward the stable door. He stumbled and nearly fell, and grasped onto a nearby stall door to regain his balance for a second. Then he struggled forward again.

He reached the stable door in time to see Iven riding out of The Oarlock's courtyard gate. Job was close behind.

Leminster and Bart were in the courtyard. Bart charged at Job, shouting for him to stop.

Job's answer was a swing of his sword that caught Bart in the shoulder. The Marshall fell, and Job's horse ground him into the mud of the courtyard as it charged out onto the street beyond.

Leminster roared in wordless rage and ran after them. He reached the street and turned in the direction the thieves had gone then stopped.

"I'll get you, you backstabbing bastards!" he shouted, and he threw the tankard he held clutched in his hand after them.

Raedrick made his way over to the Marshall, weaving with every step as he still had not fully regained his equilibrium. When he reached Leminster's side, he looked to the right and could just see Job's back as he spurred his horse away. Then he vanished into the night.

"Son of a bitch," Raedrick said.

"Will pay," Leminster added, completing Raedrick's very thought.

Raedrick looked at him, and the Marshall had murder in his eyes.

# 28

## TAKING MUSTER

Raedrick stumbled back to where Bart lay and crouched down next to him. Leminster had beaten him there, and the Marshall was checking his man over.

"Is he - ?"

Leminster shook his head. "He's alive. The cut's not too bad actually, but the horse really did a number on him. I'm afraid to move him to see how badly, though."

That much was certain. Bart lay on his belly in the mud. He was bleeding from his left shoulder where Job had cut him. His right arm was bent at an unnatural angle and he had a large lump on his head that was growing larger by the second. He also had a muddy hoof print in the middle of his lower back, and his left leg looked weirdly twisted.

He would be a long time recovering, that's for sure.

"I agree with not moving him. Better to get the Healers Circle; they can see to him if anyone can." Raedrick pushed himself to his feet and looked back at the stable. He was relieved to see Julian, his hand pressed to his head and looking a bit dazed, stumbling out toward them.

From the doorway to the taproom, a crowd had begun to spill out into the courtyard, and in the second level, lights were beginning to come on in some of the guest rooms. It wouldn't be long until everyone in town knew what happened.

Not like he was trying to keep it a secret.

He saw Molli push her way through the small crowd and called out to her. "Send someone to fetch Master Sebastini please."

She looked as though she were about to come take matters into her own hands for a second, but then she nodded and turned to the side, where one of her barmaids stood looking shocked and confused. Molli spoke into her ear for a moment, then the girl nodded quickly and darted past Raedrick and Leminster, out to the street and then in the general direction of the Guildhouse.

Julian came to a halt next to them, and for a second Raedrick thought he was going to fall over. He had a bad gash over one eye and he definitely looked dazed. But his face was a mask of determination and his eyes glinted in the lamplight. He was far from done with this fight.

"We're going after them, right?"

Raedrick nodded, but it was Leminster who spoke. He looked up from where he knelt beside Bart and said, between gritted teeth, "Damn right we are."

Julian nodded, then he stepped around Raedrick toward the gateway.

"Where are you going?"

Julian stopped and turned around to face him. "Going to get Melanie, Rae. We're going to need her."

Raedrick blinked. Melanie? Why - ?

Julian must have seen the confusion on his face. He scowled. "Iven is a bloody mage."

"Surely not. How - ?"

"Explain it to him, Caperick." Julian turned and moved with a purpose out into the street. He glanced back once. "Don't leave before I get back."

Then he hurried away into the night.

Julian pounded on Melanie's door with both fists and shouted, "Melanie! Wake up!"

No response.

He did it again, and kept on doing it continuously for at least a minute or two. In other buildings around, lights began coming on in the upper windows, and a couple of the windows pushed open and people stuck their heads out to see what was the matter.

He couldn't have cared less.

Finally, a light came on in Melanie's upstairs window. It moved through the upstairs, from one window to another, and then finally Julian saw it brighten the floor of her shop through one of the windows.

The door swung open and Melanie, clad in a nightgown with a wrap pulled over her shoulders, glared out at him. Her hair was mussed and her eyes squinted from sleepiness. Behind her right shoulder, a small glowing globe hovered, casting illumination in a wide arc around her.

"Julian, what do you think you're - " she began. Then she really saw him and her expression shifted immediately from annoyance, near anger, into a businesslike calm. "What has happened?"

"The robbers got away," he said in a rush. "One of them is a mage. We need your help."

She blinked at the flood of words and held up a hand. "Slow down. What?"

He had to force back the impulse to shove aside her question. They didn't have time to screw around. But she might just get mad and tell him to piss off. Well, she wouldn't do that. But she did need to know what was actually going on. So he took a breath, calmed himself down, and told her about Iven and the Communications Specialist program, and how he had used magic against them in the stable.

Melanie's eyebrows rose high on her forehead. "A person cannot get that level of skill in only four months, Julian."

"So? He has it. If we're going to take him down, we're going to need you with us."

She sighed and pushed one hand through her hair. "Alright. You certainly will. When do we leave?"

"As soon as you're ready..." He drifted off, just then really noticing her. Yes, her hair was mussed and she still looked sleepy. But that nightgown was...glorious. And even with the wrap around her shoulders a fair amount of her impressive cleavage was showing.

She always looked good. Beyond good. But right then she was... He didn't even know how to describe how good she looked.

And of course she saw his eyes roaming. She cleared her throat and pulled the wrap more fully closed over her chest, and gave him a level stare. But was that just a hint of a flush about her cheeks?

He spread his hands and gave a helpless little shrug, and smiled broadly, his most innocent grin. He couldn't help but look, and why should she expect otherwise? She knew how beautiful she was.

She rolled her eyes, but he thought that flush grew by a small degree. "Wait right there."

Then she shut the door in his face.

***

Master Sebastini and his two apprentices were there by the time Julian returned to The Oarlock with Melanie in tow. She was dressed for war, in a dark blue dress that had been divided for riding and was again cinched at the ankles. Over her torso, she also wore a leather harness from which danged numerous pouches, and as always she wore her belt knife. Tonight, though, a larger pouch balanced out the knife. There was a square bulge within, and Julian would have bet good money that was her book of spells. Overtop it all she wore a thick black wool cloak.

As they entered the courtyard, he considered that it was probably not fair to say she was in tow, exactly, considering she easily matched his pace and scrupulously avoided looking at him the whole way.

She wasn't actually offended that he had enjoyed looking at her. Was she?

When she saw Bart's state, though, her aloof facade cracked and she winced sympathetically. "These men have much to answer for, from the look of it."

Julian could only nod agreement.

Sebastini looked up as Melanie spoke and gave them a nod of greeting, and for Melanie a small but gentle smile. "Mistress Klemins," he said politely. "And Constable. Do you need me to look at that cut?"

Julian shook his head. "No, no. Worry about Bart."

"Yes," Melanie said, "if there's one place Julian has no fear of suffering a serious injury, it's his head."

He gave her a level look. Very funny. She returned his look with an impish grin and...stuck her tongue out at him?

Maybe he had taken more of a knock on the head than he thought; he must be seeing things.

Raedrick interrupted with a clearing throat and an incredulous stare that he directed at both of them.

Julian flushed slightly. He was right of course; it was time for business, not kidding around.

For his part, Sebastini merely smiled indulgently and got about his business. He looked at Leminster, who still knelt at Bart's side. "We will take it from here, Marshall. His injuries do not appear life threatening, but the sooner we can start treatment, the better."

Leminster nodded and rose, then backed up a pace. "Thank you, Guildmaster. If there's anything you need..."

Sebastini shook his head. "Just to let us work. You can probably see him on the morrow." He glanced from the Marshall to Raedrick, Julian, and Melanie, then added, "If you are available."

Leminster nodded, then turned away from his man. He blinked when he saw Melanie; he clearly was not expecting to see someone like her there. His eyes moved up and down her body and he grinned suddenly. "Royal Marshall Caperick Leminster, mistress..." He trailed off questioningly

Melanie rolled her eyes, and Julian couldn't blame her. Ravi *had* just said her name. "Melanie Klemins."

Raedrick interjected, "She's coming to help with the chase."

Leminster looked profoundly doubtful. He gave her another once-over, more searchingly this time. "Ah... Meaning no offense of course, Mistress Klemins, but..." He looked back at Raedrick. "Why?"

"You'll just have to trust us on this one, Caperick. We need her with us."

He looked as though he were going to press the issue, but the deadly serious tone in Raedrick's voice, or perhaps the expression on his face, apparently gave him pause. He looked back at Melanie again, then shrugged. "You say so." He straightened his shoulders. "I'll go get my gear. In the stables in five minutes?"

Raedrick nodded, and Leminster headed toward the Inn's front door. The crowd parted to let him through, and he vanished inside.

"Charming man," Melanie said. Then she sniffed and looked at Raedrick. "Julian told me the situation. I've brought tools and components that should render this Iven neutral, unless he is *truly* surprising in his ability." Her tone said she doubted he would be.

Raedrick nodded. "Let's hope we've seen the last surprise from this bunch."

Julian couldn't argue with that thought.

# 29

# PURSUIT

At least there was a good moon, a waxing Gibbous that shed plenty of light. Between that and the snow that still covered most of the ground, they were able to see quite well. All the same, why was it they always seemed to make these chases in the middle of the night? It was enough to make a man think the gods were conspiring en masse to deprive him of sleep.

At first it was obvious which way the thieves had gone; Main Street was the only road out of town that led anywhere outside of the Vale, and even after the paving on the street ended at town's edge, the road was more or less clear for a goodly way outside of town. But soon enough, they came to the intersection where the road leading to Holbart's Pass, and beyond to Mangin City, veered to the left and the road leading south past the Eastflow and then around the lake to Silver Falls and the pass to Calas beyond continued on straight ahead.

The road to Mangin city was little more than a slightly-more trampled path through the surrounding snow, hoof prints and the tracks from wagon wheels that had been left by Sarillo's caravan being the primary indication the road even existed, beyond the larger mounds of snow every few hundred yards that marked where stone distance markers were set up along the side of the road. The road to the Eastflow was even less distinct than that. Few were the tracks leading that way, but the markers still stood.

It was not immediately obvious which way their quarry had gone.

Leminster reined in and looked one way then the other, scowling.

"Do you have a notion of where they may be running to, Caperick?" Raedrick asked as he pulled his horse to a halt beside him.

Leminster shook his head. "Job has family in Pepperidge, a few days east of Mangin City. But he has to know that's the first place we would look for him."

"And Iven?" Melanie sounded decidedly curious about him. "What is his background?"

Leminster looked at her askance—he apparently still didn't know what to think about her—then shrugged. "Don't know him that well yet. He and Job go back a way, though." His scowl grew deeper. "Obviously."

Julian traded a look with Raedrick, who gave a little shrug of his shoulders then hopped down from his horse.

"Melanie, can you shed a little more light? We ought to be able to tell fresh tracks from old."

She nodded and pulled one of her pouches of components off the left side of her harness. She closed her eyes for a moment, then, emptying the pouch contents into her left hand, she voiced a quick series of unintelligible words and made a sharp gesture with her right.

A brief flash of light emanated from between the fingers of her left hand, then, dim and first but gradually growing more bright, a ball of light, just like the one that had been floating over her shoulder when she came to her door earlier, appeared in the air above her hand. She looked at it for a second and made a rising gesture, and the ball floated higher until it hovered above them all. There it grew brighter still, and in moments the area around them was illuminated as though it were early morning.

Raedrick nodded at her, a satisfied expression on his face. "Thank you."

Leminster's jaw was practically resting on his chest. He looked at Melanie with utter amazement, his eyes bulging. Little noises issued from his mouth, but he seemed unable to make actually words come forth at the moment.

Julian just smirked at him, enjoying his stupefaction immensely. "Told you," he said. He dismounted and joined Raedrick in the snow, looking at the tracks.

Behind them, Leminster seemed to have found his voice, if not his wits.

"How..." He paused, and Julian could hear him swallow nervously. "Where did you learn that? The Magestirium..."

Melanie chuckled. If he didn't know her as well as he did, he would not have caught the strain in that laugh, the way she forced its seeming confidence. "The Magestirium and I have...an understanding," she said.

That was true enough, but it was a decidedly flimsy understanding, and neither she nor he and Raedrick actually expected them to honor their side of it.

Leminster said, "Ah. I...see." But it was obvious he was baffled how a woman had been allowed to learn magecraft.

That was neither here nor there right this second, though. Julian crouched down, peering intently at a set of tracks that lead off southward toward the Eastflow. After a few seconds, he straightened, shaking his head. The tracks were weathered, by the wind and melting probably. They were not fresh.

"Over here," Raedrick said. He had been checking out the eastward road. Julian tromped over and found him pointing triumphantly at a set of tracks that lay a bit to the right of the wagon-ruts. "That's it."

"You sure, Rae? Those wagon tracks and the rest are just a couple days old." He frowned. "Looks about the same to me."

Raedrick rolled his eyes. "Look at the imprints from the horseshoes."

He bent over to look closer, and silently cursed himself for a fool, for not seeing it the first time. From the direction of the horseshoe imprints, these tracks were heading in the opposite direction as the first bunch, which had been moving westward, toward Lydelton.

Raedrick wore a smug expression as he re-mounted his horse. "Looks like your friends are going home, Caperick."

The Marshall scowled. "Not my friends," he said darkly. Then, under his breath, he added. "Not anymore."

Melanie doused her light and they pushed on. Their progress slowed considerably as their horses had to practically stomp out a fresh trail. But Julian considered that their quarry had the same difficulty, and worse for them they had not been expecting to have to flee then and were not very well equipped.

It was just a matter of time before they caught up to the thieves, and then...

He found he was gripping the reins of his horse with clenched fists. Payback was well past due for that bunch. It was bad enough that they had stolen money that could have bankrupted the entire town. But they were Royal Marshalls—or at least Iven and Job had been. Law men, sworn to uphold justice and stop criminals. For them to have taken this route was an affront to...

Well, to everything, he supposed.

Ahead of him, Leminster rode with his back stiffly erect. He was practically trembling with barely-contained rage. Julian understood completely, but for a second he couldn't help but wonder whether Leminster had any intention of taking them alive.

And would it really be so bad if he didn't?

Yes. Yes it would. Due process, and all that. They were guilty as sin, but they still needed their day in court.

When his and Raedrick's day came to answer for what

happened when they fled the Army, and he knew it would sooner or later, he would want the same.

Silently, as they rode on through the night, Julian made a point of keeping an eye on the Marshall, just in case he tried to take things too far.

## ❧ 30 ❧

## TO THE HILLS

Melanie pulled her cloak tighter about herself and wished there were a spell she could cast to ward off the cold. Although, come to think on it, there very likely was one; she just didn't know it.

It was vastly frustrating sometimes, the limits of what Timon had been able to teach her in their short time together. She had just scratched the surface, and it left her wanting more, more. Since his death, she had managed to glean a bit more knowledge here and there, but never enough. There was always something more to learn.

Her mind went to this Iven, this supposed Marshall who had trained with the Magestirium for such a brief period, but had apparently managed to learn a surprising amount. From what Julian said about their brief encounter in the stable, he had in only four months mastered, or at least become proficient with, a spell that had taken Melanie almost a year to get down, counting from when Timon first started teaching her.

And that was not even what the Magestirium supposedly set out to teach him! How had he done it?

Even if he were not the culprit behind the robbery that had so nearly crippled Lydelton, she would have set out after him eagerly, just to find out the answer to that question.

"We ought to be catching up with them around daybreak," Julian said from next to her.

Raedrick looked back from where he rode next to Marshall Leminster, skeptical. "How do you figure that?"

"They weren't planning to flee. They can't be well-equipped and they've probably been pushing their horses harder than they should. They'll tire quickly, I think."

Raedrick pursed his lips, then nodded after a moment.

From directly ahead of her, the Marshall grunted. "We'll see."

Julian grinned at their backs, and Melanie had to suppress a chuckle. He was always so happy with himself when he thought he was being clever. It was charming. And incredibly annoying.

Unbidden, her thoughts went back to that moment at her doorway, the feel of his eyes on her body when the wrap slipped. Had she somehow *meant* to do that?

Preposterous. She had no time for that sort of thing, and even if she did this certainly wasn't the time to be thinking on it.

"Get your head back in the game, woman," she said to herself.

"Eh?" Julian said, looking sidelong at her. "What was that?"

Stupid. Embarrassment flooded through her at her lapse, and she scowled at him. He recoiled, and guilt followed the embarrassment, but she pushed that aside.

He ought not have been looking, anyway.

Ahead, the road, such as it was, rose into the foothills of the Saddleback Mountains and Holbart's Pass. The moonlight, bright against the fallen snow, illuminated the scene so well she almost forgot it was nighttime.

There, ahead, on the hill, maybe two miles away. Was that movement?

"Look there," she said, and pointed, reining in.

The others stopped and followed her finger with their eyes. The Marshall grinned in vicious triumph.

"That's them," he said, and he licked his lips.

Julian and Raedrick traded a cautious look between them, after which Julian kept his eyes on the Marshall. Wary eyes.

He was not *always* foolish.

"Let's hurry," the Marshall said, and he spurred his horse to greater speed.

An hour later they crested a hill and saw something in the small valley between it and the next. Maybe a half mile away, at that distance it was only a bit of black on the blue-white of the moonlit snow. They paused atop the hill for a moment, looking around for any other sign, and finding none, proceeded down to the object.

It was a horse. Dead. From where it lay, in what looked like a pit of snow, Melanie surmised the snow had been covered a hollow in the earth, and when the horse stepped on it, the snow collapsed. The poor beast's left rear leg was broken, and the cinch for the saddle that had been on it was as well.

"Went lame and they put it down," the Marshall said, stating the obvious. He sounded satisfied, as though the horse's death was something to celebrate. "Two of them are riding double now." He glanced back at Julian. "Maybe not even at daybreak, eh?" He grinned, and then he set off along the trail of hoof prints again.

Julian and Raedrick hung back.

"He's not looking to arrest them, Rae," Julian said. "He'll just kill them if he can."

Raedrick frowned and looked up at the Marshall, now a third of the way up the next rise. Then he shook his head. "No. Caperick's a good man. He knows his duty."

"Yeah, but this is a bit beyond duty for him now. It's personal."

The frown remained on Raedrick's face as he continued to watch the Marshall climb the rise. "Then we must ensure he has no excuse to go beyond the law." He paused. "Melanie, can you ensnare them, like you did with the Out-Dweller last summer?"

She was actually impressed he thought of that. She nodded. "I brought the components. But the spell will take longer to work in the snow; the seed of the spell will have to penetrate to the earth before it can grow."

"How much longer?"

She had been wondering that herself. "I'm not sure. Anywhere from a few seconds to a minute, I think."

Julian muttered something under his breath. "That's quite a range. I'm not sure we can count on that, Rae."

Raedrick nodded. "We'll just have to keep an eye on him, help him to not go too far."

"Agreed."

They looked at each other in understanding, and all three nodded concurrence. Then they spurred their horses forward to follow the Marshall.

# JUST DESERTS

The sun had begun to peek above the mountains on the far side of the Vale, and it seemed its coming caused the land to fall silent. The breeze that had been blowing all night faded away to nothing, and as its omnipresent whistling faded the silence of the hills seemed almost deafening to Melanie's ears.

She should have known that portended trouble ahead.

The Marshall still led the way. He was approaching the crest of the hill they were climbing when he suddenly pulled his horse to a halt and waved back at the rest of them to stop as well. He remained motionless for a while, peering ahead intently. Then, slowly, he dismounted and pointed for them to do the same.

Melanie looked down at the snow, almost thigh deep on the Marshall, and then at her calf-high boots and the dress atop them, and sighed.

Beside her, Julian shook his head, but hopped down quick as can be.

The three men conferred for a moment, then Raedrick came back to her. "Caperick thinks they're just ahead, in the next valley. We're going to creep up to the summit to be sure."

She scowled. She did *not* want to get snow in her boots. But then, why had she come if she were not going to participate? This was no time to play the cringing maiden. "Very well," she said, reluctantly. Then she, too, dismounted.

The shock of the snow's cold against her legs made her hair stand on end, or seemed to. Of course she was wearing woolens beneath her dress—she was not stupid enough to go out without them—but still, it was *cold*.

But the men were not complaining, so she ought not either.

A short climb brought them to the top of the hill. They laid down on their bellies to peer over, and that sent new shivers through her body. But right away she saw that the Marshall was correct.

Down in the valley beyond their hill stood of copse of trees, evergreens mostly. It looked to be the best place to stop and rest they had seen all night, and sure enough a small wisp of smoke rose from a spot about halfway back in the copse from their position.

"Hard to think anyone else would be out here at this time," the Marshall said.

Raedrick nodded. "We diverged from the road into the pass a couple hours ago. Theirs are the only tracks."

She had noticed the lack of wagon tracks over the last few miles, and presumed that's what had happened. Did the fugitives realize what they had done? She wagered probably not.

"Well," the Marshall said, pushing himself up to his feet. "Let's go get them."

"What," Julian said, looking at him warily, "just charge straight down there?"

"You got a better idea?"

"Yeah. You two ride around to the northern side of the valley and come at them from that direction. Melanie and I will come from the south. That way if they try to run we've got them cornered."

The Marshall blinked, then looked abashed and nodded

concurrence. And he should have been embarrassed to not consider that possibility.

They remounted their horses and Julian took a moment to look back at the sunrise. "Just hitting daybreak, and we found them." He put on the charmingly annoying self-satisfied grin of his. "Who would have thought?"

She rolled her eyes, and noted Raedrick doing the same. They shared a look, and he shook his head with an amused smile. She could not help doing the same.

<br>

The smell of woodsmoke grew more intense as she and Julian picked their way through the trees. They must be getting close to the fugitives' campsite.

"Any minute now," Julian mumbled, and he eased his sword from its scabbard.

That was a good a cue as any. He knew this sort of business better than she did; if he was readying himself she ought to as well. She pulled her book of spells from its pouch and fingered the many tabs she had placed on the pages, pondering for a moment.

What would Iven do once he knew he was caught?

The better question was what *could* he do? She knew he could use force, and he had apparently more than mastered flame. What else did he keep in his repertoire?

Best to have a general counter spell ready. She flipped to that page and reviewed the incantation quickly. She knew it by heart, but it never hurt to double check, especially in situations like this. Then she removed the needed components from a pouch that hung on the right side of her harness. After another moment's thought, she pulled out the components for another little trick as well. Then she replaced the book into her pouch.

She glanced over at Julian and found him looking at her, questioningly.

"Ready?"

She nodded.

"Alright." He grinned. "Let's - "

From ahead, a shout issued forth, and the sound of stomping hooves. The others had found the camp.

"Damn it," Julian said.

They spurred their horses forward.

Thirty yards later they burst out from beneath the forest canopy into a small clearing. A campfire, small but welcoming despite its size, burned in the center of the clearing, in the middle of a circle of cleared earth. A thoroughly miserable and dejected looking fellow who had only the woolens he was wearing and not a weapon to be seen stood next to the fire, hunched over in defeat. Over to the right of the fire, two other men stood. The former Marshalls, no doubt. One was slender and held a long, thin sword in his hand. Behind him and a bit to his left stood a round dark-skinned man stood without a weapon in hand, but he wore a sword on his hip. They stood near a ragged-looking lean-to that they had constructed against a broad pine.

Their horses were nowhere to be seen, but she thought she hear a whinnying off to the right as well; they must be picketed out of sight somewhere.

Directly across the clearing from she and Julian, the Marshall and Raedrick were advancing on foot into the camp, swords draw.

"Give it up, Job," the Marshall said, nodding at the lean man with the sword. "It's over."

Beside her, Julian dismounted and advanced as well, heading toward the man by the fire. She followed suit, but hung back so she could better see the entire scene.

The two former Marshalls noted her and Julian's arrival and shifted, Iven moving a bit more to Job's left to place himself closer to them.

Job put on a show of defiance, at least. "We both know I can take you, Cap."

The Marshall snorted. "Probably. But can you can take all of us?"

"I don't need to." He glanced at his comrade, who immediately began a rapid incantation.

So. It was to be fire. Melanie voiced the counter spell and felt its components burn away a heartbeat before Iven completed his spell.

He pointed at Raedrick and a line of fire, so precise and narrow it was almost invisible, raced toward Melanie's friend. Had she not been ready with a defense it would have probably bored a hole straight through him. But as it was, she focused on it and, with a wave of her hand, the beam of fire spurted and then went out halfway between Iven and Raedrick. She then immediately began casting her other spell.

Iven's mouth dropped open in surprised shock, and his eyes roamed the clearing, coming to rest upon Melanie. Realization appeared on his face a half second before she finished the second incantation.

He was still standing there with a stupid look on his face when her blow of force struck him and knocked him into the lean-to behind them. It and he collapsed to the ground with a great clatter, and he did not get back up.

Julian charged forward toward the man next to the fire. The fellow, seeing him coming, went pale with fright, and he turned to run.

He didn't get far. Julian caught him, grabbed him by the collar of his coat, and hurled him down into the snow. Then he pressed a boot to his chest and his sword to the man's throat. "Don't even think about moving, Farley," he said, his tone making it sound like he secretly hoped Farley did just that.

Meanwhile, Job just stared at Melanie, dumbstruck. It wasn't until Raedrick and the Marshall were almost upon him that he came to himself with a little shake of his shoulders.

And came to himself he did. He darted to the Marshall's side, his movements as quick and sure as a dancer's, and his sword seemed blur, it moved so quickly. The Marshall got his sword up to block the attack, but Melanie had no idea how; she could not even see which direction it had been coming from.

Raedrick circled around the Marshall to get at Job's flank, but he spun away and retreated, keeping both men in front of him and flicking his sword first toward one then the other to keep them at a distance.

The three men continued in that manner for several seconds, Job dodging and retreating, keeping always out of the reach of Raedrick's and Caperick's weapons.

When the opening came, it was so small Melanie didn't notice it. Caperick must have over-extended or something, because one moment he was moving to his left to try to get around Job and make a strike, and the next he lay on his back after receiving Job's boot in his face.

Raedrick froze for a second when he saw the Marshall fall, his determined advance quickly halting as his expression grew more wary now that he was one-on-one against the skilled swordsman.

Job wasted no time. He came on in a blur, his sword rising, falling, then cutting from left to right and back again in one continuous movement that caused Raedrick to retreat hurriedly to avoid being cut in two.

As it was, after the flurry of blows, Raedrick's cloak and coat showed three separate cuts in the fabric, and though Melanie could not tell for sure she suspected he was bleeding from the cuts.

Raedrick retreated again, bringing his sword up into a guarding position in front of himself, and Job paused, a vicious smile appearing on his face.

He had no doubt he was the better of the two of them.

To Melanie's left, Julian breathed a curse and turned away from Farley, moving as quickly as he could in the snow to lend aid to his friend. But it was clear from the expression on his face he knew he could not get there in time to make any difference.

Job advanced on Raedrick, but this time the Constable caught his cut with his sword, and it glanced aside harmlessly even as he made a quick counter.

But Job was too quick. He spun out of the way of Raedrick's attack.

Melanie rolled her eyes. This had gone well past being tiresome. She dug into another pouch, and as she did so she recalled the first time she had fought with Raedrick and Julian. How the bandit mage Lorent had almost killed Raedrick in the end by freezing his muscles as his foe stabbed at him.

How fitting to use that spell to their benefit now.

When she looked back up, Job had pressed forward again. And again, it was all Raedrick could do to avoid being skewered.

She began casting just as Raedrick countered. Yet again, Job easily skipped backward to avoid the strike. And then, just as quickly, he bounded forward, this time thrusting toward the center of Raedrick's chest.

The Constable leapt backward and desperately brought his sword back and downward to block the thrust aside.

But he was too slow; she could tell he was going to take the hit no matter what he did. Fear for her friend suddenly gripping her heart, Melanie ran through the last syllables of the chant as quickly as she had ever spoken anything.

Job froze in mid-thrust, his muscles locking up, constricted by the spell Melanie had put on him. Instead of impaling Raedrick, the former Marshall's weapon halted mere inches from his chest.

There the two men stood for a heartbeat, confusion on Job's face; relief on Raedrick's. And then Job fell gracelessly over onto his side, the awkward angle of his stance giving way beneath the demands of gravity as his muscles remained locked in place.

Raedrick turned to look at Melanie, his eyes wide. Their gazes met, and after a moment, he inclined his head to her deeply. She returned it in kind.

To the side, Caperick groaned and forced himself up into a sitting position. He paused to rub at his quickly swelling cheek with the palm of his hand, then, with a grunt, pushed himself fully upright. He stumbled forward a half-step before he was able to fully right himself, then took a moment to survey the scene.

"Well," the Marshall said, wincing as he moved his jaw to voice the thought, "I suppose it was good you came with us after all, Mistress Klemins."

Melanie sniffed and turned away from him. He *supposed*; what a twit.

She walked over to where Iven had fallen beneath the wreckage of the lean-to. Several of the branches that had made up the structure's construction covered him, but he did not look badly hurt.

In fact, as she reached his side, he stirred and pushed himself up onto his hands and knees. He saw her boots and looked up at her, his eyes confused.

"How?"

She kicked him in the face, and he went back down. She wiped her hands on the front of her dress, removing the last residue of the used-up spell components.

Then she gave Iven one last look, sniffed, and turned away from him.

"Amateur," she said.

❧ 32 ☙

# PAYBACK

Raedrick dropped a sack onto Mayor Brimly's desk. It landed with a solid thud and the tinkle of coins striking one another—it was a beautiful sound.

The Mayor sat in his chair behind the monstrosity that was his desk and looked at the sack curiously.

"That is the four hundred marks you lent to Danil," Raedrick said before the Mayor could ask. "We figured we'd give it to you ourselves, so there was no question when the town would be repaid."

The Mayor looked askance at him, then leaned back in his chair. "No need for you to impugn Danil's character, Constable."

Raedrick just shrugged. "Just cutting out the middle man."

Brimly frowned, but he reached out and fingered the sack for a moment nonetheless. He shook his head. "I don't know how you two did it. I thought we'd never find those robbers, or get that money back if we did." He looked up at them and grinned. "Excellent work, Constables."

Raedrick inclined his head to the Mayor in response, but did not reply. There were a few things Julian thought about saying right then, but he—probably wisely—decided to keep them to himself.

Brimly swiveled a quarter of the way around on his chair, so he was looking at the room's smaller window, overlooking the side-street that ran past that side of Town Hall. "Did they say why they did it?"

Raedrick shrugged. "Does it matter?"

Brimly looked at him with a raised eyebrow. Of course it mattered.

Julian said, "Job claimed he needed the money to help his mother. Iven..." He realized he was scowling. "Leminster got a pigeon from his office this morning. Turns out there were a number of unsolved crimes in the Capital that ended around the same time he transferred. It looks as though he's been doing this sort of thing for a while. And he and Job knew each other from their early days in the Marshalls Service, so..." He left the rest unsaid.

Brimly snorted, shaking his head in disgust. "When even the men who are supposed to be upright are corrupt, what hope do the rest of us have?"

"That's a little pessimistic."

Brimly looked back at Raedrick and smiled faintly. "True enough. We have the pair of you." He stood and walked around his desk. "That's more than enough for this little town." He offered his hand to them in turn, and they shook. "Well done, gentlemen. Very well done indeed."

———

Ravi was the one who answered their knock on the Guildhouse door. That was surprising; normally it was one of the apprentices who greeted visitors.

He smiled widely when he saw them. "Ah, Constables. Welcome."

He opened the door fully and gestured for them to enter. Raedrick stepped inside immediately and stomped the slush off his boots. Julian followed more slowly. He had never really been all that comfortable in the Healers Circle Guildhouses. Something about all the sickness and injuries that congregated there.

Oh, he had all sorts of respect for the Circle for what they did, and when he had spare coin he made a point of putting some in their donation boxes—in his line of work he would need their services more than others, so it made sense even if it wasn't also the right thing to do. But that didn't mean he wanted to linger around to see people suffer.

Or, when he was really honest with himself, to think about what might happen to him one of these days.

"How are your patients, Master Sebastini?" Raedrick asked.

Ravi made a little shrug. "Marshall Wainright should recover fully. I told Marshall Leminster he'll be ready to travel in a few days." He pursed his lips slightly. "Jakob, though…" He frowned. "Hard to say."

"Can we see him?"

Ravi nodded and gestured for them to follow, then he led them back down the hallway at the rear of the Guildhouse foyer to the treatment rooms.

Jakob didn't look much better than when Julian had seen him last, except that he was bundled up in bed. His head was wrapped in a bandage and he just lay there, staring up at the ceiling, his mouth agape. It made his stomach hurt in sympathy just looking at him.

"Has he been able to say anything yet?"

Ravi shook his head. "He'll take food and water, and when we guide him he can perform basic tasks. But speech has not come yet." His tone said he doubted whether it ever would at this point.

Raedrick frowned, then stepped over to Jakob's bedside. He bent over and said softly, "We got the men who did this to you, Jakob."

Jakob twitched slightly, but he made no other response.

Raedrick sniffed softly, then straightened and looked back at Ravi with a face that was full of remorse. He smiled weakly. "I just thought he'd like to know that."

# BREAKFAST TIDINGS

The sun was just above the western mountains when Leminster and his party were ready to go.

The four prisoners—Geoff didn't get off the hook just because the Marshalls had decided to misbehave—sat dejectedly two by two in the back of a wagon, their hands shackled behind their backs and fastened to the slats that made up the sides of the wagon. Each had a blanket thrown over him, but it would not be a comfortable way to ride, regardless.

Bart sat up front on the wagon, looking exactly like a man who had been run over by a horse. His right arm was splinted in two places and hung in a sling. His left leg was encased in one long splint and bandage, and he wore a bandage over the side of his head and on his shoulder, beneath his coat. His eyes were a bit bleary from the medicines Master Sebastini had given him to control the pain, but he looked ready to go. Or as ready as he could.

Beside him sat Hiram, one of the fishing men who had assisted Julian and Raedrick in the defense of the town against Isenholf's brigands last year. He held the reins to the wagon's team in his hand and actually looked eager to be off.

Three others of the fishing men who had fought that battle

volunteered to accompany Leminster and Bart on their journey to Mangin City. Gilroy, Tomi, and Willem sat astride horses, and though they did not look particularly comfortable on the steeds, they had determined looks on their faces and bows tucked beneath their bedrolls behind their saddles. All four of them had been keeping their archery skills up, just in case.

Looked like that had been a good idea.

Leminster surveyed his party and nodded to himself, then he turned and walked over to where Raedrick stood next to Julian, at the gateway to The Oarlock's courtyard. The Marshall rubbed his hands together and smiled thinly. "Guess we're about ready to go." He paused, then added, "I wanted to thank you for your help."

Raedrick made a dismissive gesture. "No thanks are necessary. If anything, it was you who helped us."

Leminster looked at him askance. "If we hadn't come up here, your company wouldn't have been robbed. And," he swallowed, looking decidedly uncomfortable, "if you hadn't figured out who did it, I would probably be lying in a ditch somewhere between here and Calas with my throat cut."

Julian had to admit, that was a good reason for him to be thanking them. "Sorry your operation with Sarillo's caravan got screwed up."

Leminster shrugged. "The boys in Calas can continue without us. Hopefully." He didn't sound too hopeful. He paused, suddenly looking uncertain about something. He eyed the two of them, scratching at his beard, but said nothing for a long several seconds.

Julian and Raedrick exchanged a look. "Was there something else, Caperick?" Raedrick asked.

The Marshall seemed to be debating something with himself. Finally, he sighed and gave a little nod. "Wasn't going to tell you this, but considering..." He drew a breath. "During Isenholf's trial, he pulled out all the stops in his defense."

"So you said."

"Aye, I did. What I didn't tell you is near the end, when nothing else worked, he named the two of you as deserters."

Julian could not move. His bones had suddenly gone to ice, his bowels to water. Panic flooded through him, but he could not make himself do anything about it. They were found out. It was all over.

From the corner of his eye, he saw Raedrick had a similar reaction, but was probably dealing a lot better than he was.

Leminster watched the two of them closely, then nodded, as though what he saw confirmed it. And it probably did, at that. "I told the judge that was hogwash. I had met and interacted with you on two separate occasions, and you were upright men, doing well by the town and the people. Still, after the trial was concluded he directed me to look into it, desertion being as serious a matter as it is."

And now the axe would fall. Julian tried to brace himself, but was still unable to do anything but stand there and listen, poleaxed.

"I can't say I approve of some of the things you're doing up here," the Marshall said, shaking his head. "I recognize sometimes a man's gotta make the best of what he's got to work with, but all the same I think you're making no end of trouble for yourselves with that Klemins woman." He drew a quick breath. "Still, as I told you the other day, it seems like we've got a good system going here, and long as it stays that way I don't see the need to upset it."

He turned away from them and walked over to his horse.

Julian looked at Raedrick, disbelievingly. He saw that his friend had a similar expression as he must: shock, relief, and puzzlement all mixed into one.

Taking hold of the saddle horn, Leminster boosted himself up. Then he looked around at his party and made a little circling gesturing with the index finger of his right hand.

Roll out.

Hiram clucked and gave his reins a shake, and the wagon

team began to move. As it passed them by, Hiram grinned at them and nodded. Bart raised his good hand to his brow in a quick salute and also smiled.

The other fishing men rode past, and made similarly respectful goodbyes.

Leminster came last. He reined in before of them and looked their way one last time. "Fare well, Constables. I'll see you next time." He grinned then. "But not too soon, I hope." Then he spurred his horse and rode away.

"Did he just do what I think he did?" Julian said. It seemed too much to believe.

Raedrick nodded slowly. "I think so."

"Bugger me," Julian said as he watched the group ride away. "He let us off the hook." Unbelievable.

"For now."

Yes. For now. That could change in a heartbeat, if they got out of line or things started going badly up here. Or if Leminster found himself under pressure. But for the time being, it looked like they were in the clear. And that was better than nothing.

Julian grinned and clapped Raedrick on the shoulder. "Breakfast?"

"Definitely."

They went inside and selected a table near the rear of the taproom. As they were settling down, Julian realized this was the exact table they were sitting in almost a year ago, when Mayor Brimly and the late Constable Malory asked for their help in driving off Isenholf's brigands. Funny the difference a year makes.

Tami came by and dropped off two cups of water with her usual semi-teasing grin. They ordered breakfast and she hurried off, but not before giving her hips a little shake.

Julian couldn't help but laugh, at Raedrick's bemused expression as much at her antics.

"Well," he said, raising his cup in a toast. "All's well that ends well, I suppose. Here's to a job well done."

Raedrick nodded and said, "Here, here." They knocked cups

together and exchanged satisfied grins, then drank up. Right then, Julian wasn't sure that life could get much better.

A plate landed in front of him, then another landed in front of Raedrick. Quite unceremoniously. He looked up and to the left and saw Molli, clad in a rather nice flowery dress with her usual white apron overtop and a towel flung over one shoulder. She looked at them—really, at Raedrick—with a neutral expression that was a far cry from the warm smile she usually held for them.

For that matter, her eyes were…almost hostile. What the - ?

"Lani's sick again this morning," Molli said, not looking away from Raedrick for even a second.

Raedrick winced. "I'm sorry to hear that, Molli. I'll go see her as soon as - OW!"

She grabbed the towel off her shoulder and hit him over the head with it. Sounded like she hit him hard.

"She's been sick every morning for the last week. Do you know what that means?"

Readrick, apparently baffled, looked at Julian for help. Sick every day? Oh crud.

"Bad food, Rae." Julian nodded and took a deep breath. "We'll get right on that. Have to check all the stores in town, sift the good from the bad." There were all manner of problems this could cause. "Might mean a few lean weeks, but luckily the thaw should come soon, and we can - OW!"

She hit *him* over the head with the towel. Twice.

"Not bad food, you lunkhead." She looked between the two of them as though unable to believe living beings could be as stupid as they were.

Right then, Julian, baffled as he was, felt just that dumb. Where was she going with this?

Molli leaned toward Raedrick and stared hard into his eyes. "It means Lani is with child." She poked him in the shoulder with her index finger. Hard. "*Your* child." She drew herself up to her full height and stared down at him with a mixture of accusation and expectation. "I've been very patient with you, Constable, but the time for messing around is over. You need to do the right thing by her." Her eyes narrowed. "Got me?"

Raedrick bobbed his head up and down, but said nothing.

Molli sniffed and turned away. She flung the towel back over her shoulder as she made her way back to the bar.

Julian watched her go, stunned into silence for a long moment. Then he burst out laughing.

"Well hot damn, Rae," he said. "I don't know whether to congratulate you or give condolences..." He trailed off as he turned back to his friend and saw the expression on his face.

Julian had known Raedrick for years. They had fought in dozens of battles together, defied the Army when it issued them an immoral order together, fled together across hundreds of leagues with the law on their tail, faced down supernatural creatures, brigands, thieves, corrupt law men, insane mages, and magical traps.

But in all that time, he had never before seen on Raedrick's face the total, all-encompassing terror that he showed right then.

# MESSAGE FROM THE AUTHOR

Thank you for reading my book. I hope you enjoyed reading it as much as I enjoyed writing it.

Every review helps an author out, so whether you loved this book, hated it, or something in between, please take a minute to tell other readers what you thought. All of the online retailers make it very easy to do, and I would really appreciate it.

Feel free to come say hi at my website or on Gab. I always enjoy hearing from readers, especially since you all are, collectively, my boss.

I also have a weekly podcast, Story Time With Michael Kingswood, where I read stories and talk through some of the latest goings on in my world. I'd love to see you there.

Thanks again. My best to you and yours.

Warm Regards,
Michael Kingswood

# MAILING LIST

If you enjoyed this book and would like word on new releases and special deals from Michael Kingswood, sign up for his newsletter on his website. Guaranteed to be spam-free, you can opt out at any time. And you can rest assured he will not share your information with anyone, for any reason.

https://michaelkingswood.com/newsletter-signup/

# MEMBERSHIP

Michael would like to invite you to become a supporting member of his website. Similar in concept to Patreon, a few dollars a month will give you access to exclusive content, and help him to focus more of his time to writing fun and exciting stories for your enjoyment.

Sign up at his website:

https://www.michaelkingswood.com/membership/join/

# ABOUT THE AUTHOR

Michael Kingswood is 20-year veteran of the US Navy submarine force and a lifelong fan of science fiction and fantasy literature. His work has appeared in numerous collections and anthologies, to include the Fiction River Anthology series from WMG publishing. He holds a bachelors degree in Mechanical Engineering as well as a Master of Engineering Management and a Master of Business Administration. He has four children and currently resides in San Diego.

Find Michael Kingswood online at:

www.michaelkingswood.com

www.facebook.com/michael.kingswood

twitter.com/michaelkingswd

DAWN OF ENLIGHTENMENT

Masters Of The Sun

---

NOVELLAS

What Lurks Between

The Necromancer's Lair

The Champion

Veritas Morte

---

STORY COLLECTIONS

Stories From The Great Challenge

Tales Of Adventure #1

Tales Of Adventure #2

Short Story 10-Pack

A Jar Of Mixed Treats

Short Mystery 10-Pack

Stories From Glimmer Vale, Volume 1

---

SHORT FICTION

Michael has also published a number of shorter works, links to which can
be found on his website.